Lupine Investigation

By Harlowe Frost

Coastal Wolves

Dedication:

I am amazed I wrote a full series and got all the books published in a year. I'm sure my editors are wanting to hunt me down at this point, but I love them to pieces, and they know that. I wouldn't be the writer I am today without the love and support of Wes Imrisek and Angela Grimes. They've always seen in me a storyteller with tales others want to read. They've seen past my dyslexia and grammar mishaps to the worlds I want to explore.

The three of us work on books together and laugh when we lose words, as all writer do. Somehow, we have a series of jokes around the living room. Angela read a few lines I wrote about a seat that sat just two people comfortably. She asked ... do you mean a loveseat? Wes challenged me when I declared some couches were for sitting and other were not. Actually, this one we still debate about. If ever you see me go on about couches, you now know why.

I have an alpha reader, Nicole Maness, who reads my stories almost before I finish writing them. She and her wife comb through my writing in its rawest form. She'll sometimes challenge me with things she sees in memes. That's where the shirt that fell with a crash ... with Caroline in it ... came from in book 6. There is a bit in this book as well. I love these challenges; it amuses me to find ways to creatively incorporate her suggestions into the stories.

As I mentioned before, I have some ARC readers, people who get advanced copies of my books. They leave lovely reviews right away. Shimere Alexander, Betsy Tilton, Elle Armstrong, Louise Morelli, and others.

Though writing is a solitary activity, it takes a village to get a book into the hands of readers, and I am truly blessed with my village.

Chapter 1 - A Wedding On The Beach
Tamsin

The wrought iron arbor, covered in flowers and magical symbols meaning peace, love, and longevity, attracted the seagulls. As did the tables, which groaned under the weight of all the food piled on them. People danced across the beach with abandon.

In the center of the dancing was Maria in a white, form-fitting dress, with flowers and lace highlighting her curves. She danced with Blake, wearing a white crop-top and matching skirt that flared when she twirled. They looked happy and beautiful together. Both elegant and hippie at the same time.

I wonder if Paige and I could elope and just have a post-wedding celebration like this? It seems so much less stressful. All the planning we're doing is awful.

The most entertaining couple tottering around in the sand was Stewart and Rainy, the resident six year olds, in their flower-person attire. They both wore light blue button-down formal shirts that went to their knees. They wore them as dresses with belts that kept tops in place. The two bounced and gyrated with the best of wolves and witches flowing around the dance area. They'd almost taken out three adults as they moved around the beach to the music.

Tamsin sat at a table, watching as everyone enjoyed the beautiful weather by the ocean. She and Joyce had disagreed about where this celebration should take place, but in the end, Joyce had been correct. Her daughter's wedding celebration needed the space the beach provided.

Warm hands slid around Tamsin's shoulders, and she leaned her head back against Paige. The other woman nearly purred. "Look at all of this. You did it, you know. You healed your people, brought these groups together, and made all of this possible."

"Hmm. You think?"

"I don't think, Tam, I know. I saw it happen over the last several months. Your strength and love. It's what this town needed."

Tamsin snorted. "How much have you had to drink, love?"

One of the warm hands slipped away, and her shoulder was soundly punched. "Ha, ha. We should dance."

Cinthia approached from the throng of people, a smile playing across her face.

"Let's give it a few more minutes, and then I'm yours for the night."

"Just the night?" Paige teased.

"For as long as you want me."

She leaned down and kissed Tamsin behind her ear. "Better."

Cinthia, an older woman who looked like everyone's favorite aunt, wore a patchwork ankle-length skirt, a blousy light blue shirt with ties at the wrist, elbow, neck, and waist, and a scarf around her waist. With a welcoming smile she took the seat next to Tamsin. "This is wonderful. I'm so happy for those two. I knew the moment I saw them together they'd be perfect for each other."

Tamsin narrowed her eyes. "I wonder about you and your ability to read auras. Can you always play matchmaker so easily?"

"Oh, it's nothing, dear. I only sometimes read people. Most of what I do is like what you do."

"Uh-huh."

"Speaking of, we should discuss Sage."

Tamsin tensed, all the good will seeping out of her. A week earlier, at the full moon run, Caroline, a witch who'd been bitten and somehow hadn't lost her magic—an anomaly if ever there was one—told her she'd discovered Sage was a black witch. Tamsin's first instinct had been to rush out and eliminate the threat. Her second had been to call Cinthia and strategize, the wiser approach.

She let her gaze sweep over the dancers again. She found Caroline dancing with a beautiful brown haired woman, another wolf. This one wasn't one of Tamsin's. Mazzy had driven in from the Colorado research group to set up a remote lap and help synthesize the antidote to the black witch concoction killing people in Santa Cruz. It had taken the genius of both Caroline and Mazzy to find the answer, and for a while, no one was certain a solution was possible. Mazzy'd only been in town for a few days. From what she understood, the woman didn't like crowds.

After Tasmin and Cinthia had discussed Sage and the black witches ... a long call, they'd decided to let the woman live, for now. They needed to find all the black witches in town. So far, every time one was discovered, they'd either ended up dead, or they disappeared. Sage was the first black witch they knew about who was still alive; they needed to use that to their advantage.

She only lives because she doesn't know we know about her. One false move and she'll probably disappear like the rest of them. Tamsin's sour mood worsened.

She sighed. "How should we do this? You said Sage had been friends with Caroline. Not a surprise—everyone likes her—but now that she's living with a wolf, I doubt Sage will be dropping by."

Cinthia laughed. "No, that avenue is no longer available. It was gone as soon as Caroline agreed to work with your pack on that serum." Cinthia paused to watch Stewart and Rainy bump into Maria and Blake and the four collapsed into a laughing heap in the sand. She smiled and then continued. "I have another witch I'm thinking about. She's relatively new to the coven. She moved to Santa Cruz last summer. Originally, she lived in L.A., but the main client she works with wanted to relocate, so they both came here."

"Her client?"

"Oh, didn't I mention? She's a personal shopper."

Tamsin's jaw dropped open, and she felt Paige behind her shaking in silent laughter. "A what now? Is she ... trustworthy?" Tamsin wanted to ask if she was clever enough, but this seemed the safer route.

Cinthia's face lit up. "Oh, yes, I think she's perfect!"

Chapter 2 - Job Roulette
Rho

R ho's phone rang. She checked the display. With a groan and a chuckle, she flopped onto the couch in her small apartment living room and answered. "Heya, Veronica. Anything crazy coming up? Need my help?"

She hadn't spent time with her socialite boss in a few weeks. The young lady had been suspiciously quiet. Rho had spent her time studying the new Power of Seven magic recently introduced to the coven. She wasn't great at the practice, but it was interesting.

"Can't I just call you, Ronny?" Veronica's slightly nasal voice pulled her from her thoughts. It always sounded like it squeezed through the phone. The woman was in her twenties, but she played at being younger, starting with her voice. "We're friends, right?"

She wanted to say, 'no.' She liked her boss, but wouldn't want to hang out with her during her free time. Every time Veronica said 'Ronny' she wanted to poke her ears out, but if the first dozen corrections hadn't worked, nothing would. The debutant loved having her own special nickname for Rho.

It was bad enough her parents insisted on calling her by her full name: Rhonda. Most people didn't even know her full name. They only knew her as Rho, and she liked it that way. She was pretty sure she'd been named after a Beach Boys song from a million years in the past. As a kid, all my teachers kept singing 'Help me Rhonda'. *If I hear that one more time, I won't be responsible for the outcome!*

She bit back a sigh and tried to keep her voice neutral, it would be a bad idea to alienate her boss. "Of course we're friends."

"Great!" Veronica's response came quick and high pitched. Rho felt bad for her negative thoughts. She needed to be a better person. "So, we can go shopping together to find me an outfit for this party? It's going to be ... I can't even. It's going to be up in San Fran and *everybody's* going to be there. I need something to wow!"

And there it was. "Sure." Rho put her phone on speaker and quickly double-checked her calendar. "Tuesday?"

Veronica squealed, and Rho shivered. "I'll have my driver pick you up at noon. We'll have lunch."

It took another few minutes to get off the phone. Rho liked Veronica, she was a good person to work for, fun to be with ... usually. She was just ... a lot.

After putting the appointment in her phone, Rho got up and took the few steps to the kitchen, wanting tea. Her apartment had a living room, a kitchen, and a bedroom big enough for a queen sized bed. The bathroom had a soaker tub, a gift from her landlord after the last renovation. Nothing in the place was large, but it suited her and her needs. More than that, she loved it.

Rho put a kettle of water up to boil, found her favorite mug, a large green mug in the shape of a cauldron with a pixie on it, and added chamomile and mint teas into a tea ball. Once the water was ready, she filled the mug, and headed to a desk in her room next to her bed to put the final notes on her last case.

Working with Veronica wasn't her only job. She had a second job none of her friends knew about as a private investigator. She used a pseudonym to help her move around more easily. The only person who knew about her true vocation was Cinthia, her coven leader. Before moving to California, she'd worked with her dad and learned all the tricks of the trade from him.

Overall, she was doing well as an investigator, just like her dad back in Texas. She had a good reputation. Word of mouth amongst her clients did more than any advertising. There were a few prospects she needed to sort through for her next job. She kept her notes on all her cases in her desk in a locked drawer.

At the desk, she'd summarized each job, something she usually did at the end of the case. They were all comparable in projected effort they would take to solve and the income they'd generate. None of the files interested her, they were all the same types of jobs she'd been doing, simple, unchallenging, beneath her. She debated putting them in a cap and randomly drawing one out, or just throwing a dart at one.

As her mind spun, she used a push of her air magic to lift a pencil and have it rotate above her hand, faster and faster with her thoughts. The ring of her phone interrupted her, and the utensil soared onto her bed.

She glared at the pencil in frustration. "For fuck's sake, Veronica, what do you want now?" She pulled her phone from her pocket and answered it without checking the display. "Veronica?"

"Um ... no? It's Cinthia, dear. Could you come over to the coven house? We need to talk."

Chapter 3 - Chasing a Lead
Ziry

The wind cut through her fur and a shiver ran down her body. All around her, the sun reflected off the snow, practically blinding her with the brightness. *How is the sun so bright and the temperature so bloody cold? Damn it! I'm a wolf. Fuck the snow, I can handle this!* Her defiance didn't block the next sharp blast of Canadian wind that tried to knock her down.

The game in this area had cut a path through the snow, so she wasn't sinking, but the scents distracted her. A family of coyotes ran this path regularly. She could smell a large cat. Nothing she could hunt on her own. *Hunt? I'm out here on a job! I should've had a larger breakfast. Who knew I'd be running today?*

Stupid job! Why did I agree to doing this? It's below my abilities. Silly, stubborn, pain in the ass Dotty, hired me to prove her husband is cheating. Ziry couldn't see it. As overbearing and intense as Dotty was, Henry loved his wife. He doted on her. Everyone in the pack knew it. Gah! *I'm a fucking detective. Why is Dad bringing me these awful cases? Is it a test of how I'll work with the annoying elements in the pack?*

Ziry had two brothers, but she was next in line to run the South Dakota pack. She'd proven her ability to organize, problem solve, and lead. *But have I shown myself to be a people person? Will the others respond to my leadership?*

She yipped in amusement at her own thoughts.

Both her brothers were charismatic but didn't have any of the other necessary alpha qualities, including power. That was it, Dad needed to see her lower herself to help Dotty with this job well beneath Ziry's skills.

Rabbit-scent perfumed the air, and Ziry's stomach snarled its approval. Veering off course, she slowed, having to tromp through snow that tickled her belly. She followed the delectable smell. She found the beast, unusually fat for January, munching on a persistent winter branch. Ziry froze, then inched forward, glad that the weather had been warm enough that the snow didn't crunch under her weight. The frozen ground cover didn't have the hard layer of ice that would either support her or give her away. Instead she plowed through the powdery cold drifts like sand on a beach.

Ziry silently pounced. She caught her lunch, and with a decisive shake of her maw, snapped the rabbit's neck. Crouching, she quickly ate, then bounded off towards the trail and her target.

After a few minutes, she reached the lake's edge. In the center was a small red fishing tent, smoke rising from the roof. Ziry closed her eyes and listened. She could just hear two people talking.

Henry, the ass, wasn't alone! Dotty was right, he was cheating. She rubbed her nose on her paw in annoyance. *I didn't want her to be right!*

"Hold it steady. That's good. Yes!" Henry's voice echoed over the smooth surface of the icy lake.

"Like this?" Ziry shook her head. The voice was male. *Why, Henry, what have you been hiding?*

"Deeper." Henry corrected. "Yes, mmm," he hummed. "That's perfect."

There were a few beats where Ziry couldn't hear anything. She debated leaving, but she didn't have enough proof. She needed to know who the other person was. She couldn't identify his voice yet.

"Yes! Got it!" She still couldn't place the voice. *Is he pack? Was that a splash?* "I'm still confused about what we're doing out here, Henry."

"It's the fish."

Ziry wanted to mouth 'fish,' but her wolf couldn't show her confusion. Her mind stuttered on what two men did with fish. She wasn't sure she *wanted* to know.

The other man helped her out. "Can't you just take this home, cook it there?"

Cook? Ziry had to stop herself from making a noise. For fuck's sake, they were really ice fishing? And cooking their catch?

"Of course I can't. If I do, Dotty will insist on cooking it, and she'll ruin it. I love her, and she can cook most things, but she ruins fish, and you know it's my favorite," he whined. His companion chuckled softly at his obvious chagrin. "I crave it and can't get out here to fish as much in winter. We'll just cook this right quick and eat it. Well, you'll cook it, you're amazing with fish. Then I'll go home, and no one will be the wiser."

Ziry's head dropped. The asshole wasn't cheating on his wife. He was cheating on her cooking.

Chapter 4 - Make New Friends ...
Rho

After getting off the phone with Cinthia, Rho cleaned up her desk, locking away all the papers for her private investigation work. The likelihood of someone stopping by was low, but it was never zero, so she always locked things away.

While she cleaned, and then during her drive to the coven house, she contemplated how she got to where she was now.

Rho left her family and their coven in Texas five years ago. She wanted to move to Los Angeles and see what life had to offer. On a particularly hot day, she'd been getting new clothes that said LA more than San Marcos, Texas, when she ran into Veronica, a socialite. The young woman had been trying to find party clothes, but her eye for fashion ... wasn't. She was getting better, but at the time, she'd needed a lot of help.

Though, while living in Texas, Rho had been active in her local coven, when she'd moved to LA, she didn't seek out her witch sisters. She practiced on her own. She didn't mind being a solitary witch, but she enjoyed having other witches around.

When Veronica called her crying that she had to move to Santa Cruz with her modeling company, Rho debated. She finally decided she could start over again.

After she arrived in Santa Cruz and settled into her new apartment, she went to buy veggies at the open air market. She ran into Cinthia, who invited her to a coven meeting. She really looked up to

Cinthia and her ability to grow such a strong group. Being with them felt like coming home, especially after three years of working magic on her own. Over the last two years, she'd quietly become a pillar among the other witches.

Despite how integrated she was in this coven, if her work took her somewhere else, she knew she'd probably move. Considering she was in her mid-thirties, she should settle down and stop flitting about like a butterfly, but she liked the idea that she could spontaneously move on a whim.

I can grow up later.

She parked and headed up the stairs to the beautiful Victorian house. Inside, she entered a great room combining a living space, kitchen and dining area. Usually, she found Cinthia in the kitchen, cooking up a storm. Today, she sat at the dining table with two steaming mugs of tea and a tray with cheese, crackers, and dip. It looked like spinach and artichoke dip.

"Rho! You made it. Come sit. I'm so glad you're here." Cinthia's smile warmed her to her soul. With the greeting, she pushed one of the steaming mugs over. The scent of peppermint filled the air.

With an effort, Rho relaxed her stiff hands. "I'm not used to you calling me in for meetings. I feel like I'm being called into the principal's office. Everything okay?" Rho smiled back, letting Cinthia know she was kidding.

"Of course. Are you hungry? Have you eaten? I can whip up something more substantial than this."

Rho sat and picked up a piece of cheese, popping it into her mouth. She wrapped her hands around the mug and let the heat warm her cool fingers. "This looks perfect. So, what's up?"

Leaning back, Cinthia brought the tea mug up to her nose to smell the relaxing scent, before taking a sip. "You know about the hullabaloo with the black witches and the spell they've netted over the city, right?"

Confusion swirled in Rho's gut. *Does she think I'm a black witch?* "Um, yeah. I've heard about that concoction they've brewed, but hasn't Caroline and her new wolf friend, what's-her-name, figured out a solution?"

Cinthia's smile widened. "Yes, Caroline and Mazzy figured out how to counter the black magic. Mazzy is working on getting a lab opened up in town so she can get enough of the cure, which also works as a counter-compound."

"Excellent, but that still doesn't explain what I'm doing here."

"Before Caroline left to work with Mazzy and the other wolves in Colorado, Sage trusted her."

A shiver went down Rho's back. "Sage is ... an odd duck. I don't know what it is about her, but she's ..." Rho grimaced. "Uncomfortable."

"How much do you feel that way?"

Rho narrowed her eyes as she selected a cracker to dip in some spinach dip. "Why do you ask?"

Cinthia leaned forward, placing her mug back on the table. "Well, we've determined that she's one of the black witches who came into town. We aren't sure why they're here, except to destroy the coven and the pack and take over our territory. We're not sure of the rationale for killing the norms. And we don't know how many are here. One of the witches was arrested a while back, and he ended up dead before anyone could question him." One of her eyebrows rose.

Dread and excitement warred within Rho. "Wait, do you want me to friend Sage and try to suss out all her deepest darkest secrets?" At Cinthia's smile, she continued. "You're asking to hire me."

"Yes, dear. I know you're very good at what you do. I thought that if you befriended Sage, you could possibly get information from her, do some investigation. If not names, then maybe locations. There are other black witches in town, a lab, homes, any number of things. We need to know that so we can put an end to what they're doing."

"And we don't know any of their end games?" Curiosity gnawed at Rho.

"I don't, and in the end, we're talking about black witches. They're dangerous. You're my first choice for this because I think you'll be great, but at the same time, my insides get tied up with fear for you."

Warmth filled Rho at the love she felt for and from her coven leader. "I'm just befriending Sage so I can poke around, right? It isn't like I'm telling her I want to join the dark side." Rho snorted as Cinthia laughed.

With a nod, Cinthia said, "I'm not the only one with information. There'll be a meeting here tomorrow night, if you want to come. See how much more information we can get."

The thrill of a new job superseded the dread of having to spend time with her least favorite witch. "Tell me when, and I'll come back! Should I bring something to share?"

Chapter 5 - Gathering the Guard
Tamsin

"Who all will be there?" Paige asked. She stood from the bed they shared while the ensuite bathroom in the alpha domain of pack house got remodeled. Moving to the dresser, she bumped into the small desk and chair they had installed for all the paperwork they both had.

"Damn it, every morning. This remodel will be worth it, but the bruises may be permanent." She started rummaging through the drawers. "I get that guests will come and deserve the bigger rooms, but with all your school papers, alpha papers, and my journalism work, we barely fit."

Turning with her outfit, she tripped on a suitcase and fell onto the bed with a squeal. Tamsin chuckled.

"We'll be fine in here." She leaned down and kissed her fiancé's forehead before Paige rose to strip off her sleepwear. "As for who will be there, I'm not sure." Tamsin kept her focus on her mate as she dressed; it was the best show in town. Paige's beauty had captivated her since they'd first met. No one else compared to the lithe and sexy woman as she slipped into jeans and a T-shirt. It didn't matter what she wore, Tamsin always wanted to tear the clothes back off and have her way with the woman.

No time for that now. Later. She shook her head, bringing herself back to the conversation at hand. "Cinthia said she wanted to introduce us to the witch who'd be helping deal with Sage." Tamsin growled when she said the name of the traitorous black witch. Her hands fisted, as if squeezing the stick-like neck of the evil bitch. It took all her control not to end the evil instantly. "But if I were to guess, they'll be more there than just the two of them."

Finally dressed, Paige came over and gave her a quick kiss. As her mate, the kiss had her mind thinking naughty thoughts. As a submissive wolf, her touch calmed her. "Come on, let's head out before we're dragged into a pack debate over dinner."

Tamsin sighed. "I've had enough debates with the discussions with my students today. The semester just began, but I have a few students who are really opinionated."

They decided to head down the back stairs which led to the garage. The drive over to the coven house was quick. Once there, Tamsin took a moment to mourn her aunt and uncle. After selling the house to Cinthia and the witches, they'd built up the garden. Colorful flowers and a bounty of plants, herbs, and flowers grew in the side yard. Tamsin realized the witch's magic helped with the abundant growth, but the sight hit her hard. Her aunt didn't have the magic to help her garden, and she put in blood, sweat, and tears for the tiny plot she'd cultivated. She'd have loved what it was now, but it was a reminder of everything that had changed.

Tamsin turned her attention to Paige as her hands squeezed the steering wheel. Even before they'd met, Paige had loved her aunt and uncle, too. They'd been her neighbors. The loss was important to both of them. It had been over a year since her uncle had been killed in a dominance fight, but the one year anniversary of her aunt's death was coming up, close to her and Paige's wedding date.

Thinking about her family, a small smile tugged across her face. She realized that Aunt Elinor would be thrilled with all the changes that had happened in Tamsin's life, starting with putting down a problematic alpha, to taking over the pack, and finally finding love. It amazed her that a year ago she was a lone wolf in Chicago, hiding under the radar, and now ... gah! So many changes.

Paige reached over and gave her hand a squeeze. "I know, I miss them, too. I really loved your family. Maybe we can have a remembrance on the one year anniversary with the pack. Maybe out on the beach. I bet a lot of them would really like that. Something to remember both Clyde and Elinor."

Fighting her tears, Tamsin nodded. She loved how well Paige understood her.

They got out of the car and headed up the steps. The house was no longer hers, no longer part of her family, but she knew that Aunt Elinor would approve of the coven owning it. The house exuded magic, it was in its bones.

They knocked, and Cinthia answered. "Welcome. Tamsin, Paige, enter in peace."

Tamsin bowed her head. "Thank you, Cinthia. I enter in peace and hope for nothing but tranquility for you and yours."

Behind her, Paige said, "I wish you peace and tranquility."

Inside, sitting on the couches in the living room, were Caroline, Mazzy, and a woman with short brown curly hair wearing a stylish green wrap dress with a black belt. Tamsin recognized her from previous visits. She wasn't sure of the woman's name, but she knew she was a witch, not only from her herbaceous scent, but because she was always at coven events when Tamsin was invited.

Caroline leapt up and gave Tamsin a hug. "Hi! I missed you at school today. I would've told you I was coming if I'd've seen you. I have been so involved in all of this—both Mazzy and I have—that we just wanted to stay in the loop."

Tamsin squeezed her back. Caroline, long-time witch, and latest wolf to join her pack, had instantly become a friend when they'd met. She was a hard person to dislike. "No worries. I had a feeling it was going to be more than just the four of us." Tamsin faced Mazzy. "Nice to see you. Hope you're enjoying our town."

Mazzy grinned. "I like the warmer weather. The lack of snow in January is thrilling. And the lab set-up is progressing well."

"I bet. Colorado is a beautiful state, but, like Chicago, cold in winter." Mazzy joined her in a small laugh.

Cinthia waved towards the third person in the room. "Tamsin, Paige. I'd like to introduce you to Rho. She's relatively new to the coven. I think your aunt used to complain about us needing to train all the new witches. Well, she knows her magic, it's just the meshing with the group we had to work on."

Tamsin narrowed her eyes. "Is this the personal shopper?" She made a closer inspection. Rho had a bag sitting on the table. It looked designer and matched her shoes. Earrings and a necklace completed the outfit. She looked understated and well put-together.

A smile broke out across the woman's face, and it lit the room. "That's me, shopper extraordinaire. Anything you're looking for?"

Paige stepped forward, a smile on her face as well. "As it goes, yes. Wedding dresses."

Tamsin groaned, and everyone else in the room laughed.

Rho patted the couch next to her. "Sit, we'll talk, but first let's get the Sage issue out of the way."

"Perfect," Tamsin said, voice droll. "Can you explain why a personal shopper is the right choice to befriend someone dangerous?"

Paige sat next to Rho while Cinthia poured tea from a kettle placed on the table between the couches. There was milk, cream, and sugar available for people to adjust their tea as they chose. Also on the tray was a selection of small sandwiches and cookies.

Rho's face grew serious. "I don't often discuss my primary occupation." She licked her lips and took a deep breath. "I *am* a personal shopper, but I'm also a private investigator. I've been in that profession since before leaving Texas." She smoothed out the skirt of her dress as she finished her statement.

A sense of relief filled Tamsin. She now understood Cinthia's confidence. "Do you feel that this is something you can do alone?"

"Yes and no. I know I can probably get close to Sage. We've spoken a few times, and it's always been pleasant, but if I start doing a lot of snooping in other areas and she catches me, then the game's up. It would be better if there were more people available who know the ropes. If you can't find anyone, I can do it all. I've done this type of investigation before; it'll just take longer. With the black witches out there killing people, I'd rather this get resolved as quickly as possible."

Tamsin's respect for the P.I. increased. Her answer came out unapologetically and confidently. She knew her business and her limitations. "I can send out an email to the pack alphas. I don't know if any of the wolves out there are investigators, but it's a place to start."

Cinthia leaned back in the wing-back chair she'd sat in. "If that doesn't work, I can try to search within the witch communities, but we're not as centralized as you wolves."

Caroline smiled at everyone. "Well, it sounds like we have a plan. Who's up for a game of cards?"

Chapter 6 - An Olive Branch
Rho

The best part of Rho's apartment was a small wrought iron balcony. It wasn't huge, just big enough for a comfortable chair and a table to accommodate a tablet and a drink. This morning it held a steaming mug of coffee.

During her shopping trip with Veronica on Tuesday, the other woman had talked about this new group up in San Francisco she wanted to start hanging out with. Rho knew what that meant; it was the same thing that had happened about six months before they'd relocated to Santa Cruz. The difference was, Rho felt more at home in her small apartment than she ever had in the bustling city down south.

She shook her head and put that thought aside. *No reason for putting the cart in front of the horse.* With a few flips of her finger, she found Veronica's number. The other woman picked up on the second ring. "Ronny! Heya! It's so early, what's up?"

Rho double checked the time. It was just after eleven. Her dad's words came back to her. *A client can always hear when you're smiling or scowling, so make sure you know what your face is doing, even over the phone.*

She plastered a smile on her face. "Hi, Veronica. I was thinking about what you said, you know, about spending more time in San Fran—"

"Oh!" she interrupted. "Don't worry. I'm not dragging you anywhere. At least, not any time soon. I have a lease, you know."

"Right, I get it." Rho rubbed her temples. She just wanted a quick conversation. That was possible. The decade between their ages was showing more and more. "I just thought I could go shopping tomorrow and get you a few extra outfits, you know, in case you have a last minute engagement."

"Oh!" Her voice came through the line quieter than normal. A nice respite from the usual nasal tone. "That would be amazing. I'm busy tomorrow, but, yeah, I need some high-fashion outfits. And a pig-themed outfit."

Rho shook her head, unsure she understood that last bit. "A what now?"

"It's a fundraiser for a vegan farm, and everyone is dressing in high-fashion animal-inspired outfits. I was assigned the pig."

"But, Veronica, you eat meat."

"I know, but so do a lot of the people going. We'll just be vegan for the day. It'll be amazing!"

"Got it. A few event outfits and a pig-inspired party frock."

"You're the best, Ronny! Talk to you next week."

Rho released a huff of air, leaning back, and shutting her eyes. The coffee smoothed the rough edges of the conversations. *I swear that woman is getting worse by the month.*

After rubbing her eyes, she prepared for her next call. Again, it was picked up right away.

"Hello? Rho? Is it you?"

"Hi, Sage. I know I've never called you, I just ... I don't know many of the coven sisters and, well, we're close to the same age, sort of."

A warm laugh traveled through the line. "I hear ya. The other witches in the coven are great, but it seems the others are either older or younger."

Rho let out a huff of air. "Yeah, that." Tension ran through her body, and she released a bit of magic to ease her mood. She'd hung a rainbow of streamers around the edge of the ceiling, and as the breeze circled the room, a kaleidoscope of colors spun above her. "Anyway, between being new in town and my crazy job, I just was thinking we could talk ... or you know, watch crazy baking shows. Whatever you like."

Another laugh. "You like baking shows?"

Rho lowered her voice. "I sometimes think I should carry a knife around and test if things are randomly cake."

This got a guffaw from Sage. "That's hilarious! I love that show. We should watch it, I have some time tomorrow if you do. We could order pizza."

"No, I have to go shopping tomorrow."

"Shopping?"

"Yeah, that's actually part of the reason I called. Cinthia mentioned you like fashion. You know I'm a personal shopper, right?"

"I think I heard that about you. You work for that silly woman, right?" She sounded skeptical. Rho didn't blame her, Veronica was a bit of an obnoxious person to work for, but she did like the excuse to buy expensive clothes ... even if they were for someone else.

"Yes. But on days like tomorrow, I get to shop without her."

"Huh."

Rho laughed. After a few seconds, Sage joined in. "So, as it goes, I swear my client is getting loopy. I need to find a pig-inspired frock. You could come shopping with me, if you're interested. Company would make the whole outing more amusing than awful." Rho tried to keep her voice light and ironic. She wanted Sage to think of her predicament as amusing. Then again, it was pretty hilarious. *A pig outfit!*

"A pig outfit?" Sage sounded as flummoxed as Rho felt. "That's ... amazing. I'm not going to lie. That is one of the best requests I've heard in a while." She laughed, a relaxed sound. "Yes, absolutely. Let's go shopping for pig clothes tomorrow. We'll have to take a rain check on the show, because that *will* happen."

Rho smiled. The other woman was bad news, but the conversation had promise. "Perfect. How about we meet for lunch and go from there."

Chapter 7 - Take the Bull By The Horns
Ziry

Ziry's hand slapped down on her alarm before she was fully awake. She rubbed the crusty sleep from her eyes and then cracked them open. The glowing numbers confirmed just how early it was. With a groan, she pushed herself from her warm bed, and flipped on the light.

Squinting, she found exercise clothes, and yanked them on.

Stupid waking up early to work out. I'm a wolf, not a cat! She wasn't sure if she'd be happier if Tony were or weren't awake. Strangling him may be worth it. It was particularly cold this morning.

She made her way to the kitchen and grabbed a metal water bottle. After filling it with water, she headed to the basement and the full exercise room the pack alphas had built years ago. The only thing it lacked was a running track.

In a cupboard, she found her current goals and got to work. Tony, her youngest brother, had gone to school to study personal training, and he'd put together goals for any pack member who wanted them. Ziry wasn't sure if she appreciated the work he'd done for her or hated it, but in the end, it made her faster and stronger.

Today's workout began with a cardio warmup, then twenty minutes of cardio and weights in intervals. Then a quick cardio and stretching cooldown. Though the gym was large, she liked working out before anyone else was up, so she had the space to herself.

I'm a loner to the end. She snorted at the thought. The future alpha, a loner. Ha!

Once done, she ran back up to her room, grabbed clean clothes, then went to the bathroom to shower.

Back in the kitchen, she found her parents. Dad stood at the stove making hashbrowns and eggs. His auburn hair was starting to gray, though it still covered his head. Ziry shared his hair color and green eyes.

Ziry could smell bacon baking in the oven. Mom sat at the table, drinking a mug of coffee. She was the odd duck of the family with blonde hair and brown eyes. She smiled. "Morning, Ziry. Plans for the day? It's Saturday, you know. You *are* allowed to sleep in."

Ziry shrugged. "I like getting my workout in before I'm awake enough to know what I'm doing. Tony keeps upping all my numbers, and when I do it early, I have less urges to murder him. And, hey, if I *do* give in to my instincts, he'll be asleep, and I'll more likely get away with it."

Mom laughed as Ziry poured herself coffee. She sat across from Mom, the two watching Dad as he moved around the large kitchen, preparing a feast. Over the next few hours, many of the pack members would be in and out, eating in small groups. What he cooked wouldn't feed everyone, but it would satisfy the first wave. Someone else would prepare the next metric ton of food in a few hours.

Dad placed a few platters of food out on the table, and the three of them filled plates and started to eat.

Once they'd finished their first serving, Dad leaned back and sipped his coffee. "Ziry, I know you're ready to take over the pack."

She froze. Taking over the pack was a future goal, not today. "Dad, I do want to be alpha one day, but you and Mom are still young."

He guffawed. "We're not, but we're still strong. You've been doing well helping out the pack. You didn't mock either Dotty or Henry about their kerfuffle last week."

Ziry rolled her eyes. "I didn't. They're pack, and they had an issue." She tried not to sound flippant. "But I'd really like to work on a bigger case. It's been awhile since I've been given anything that's stretched my abilities."

The smile that spread on Dad's face worried her. "I hoped you'd say that."

She narrowed her eyes at him. Dread over his words warred with excitement at the prospect of a challenging job. "Oh?"

"I received an email from the alpha from the Pacific Pack in Santa Cruz. They have a group of black witches in town." He finished his plate of food, leaning back with his mug of coffee.

Shock sent chills down her back. "Like what happened to us all those years ago? Is their pack okay?"

His face screwed up. "Yeah, it is. I guess it was hit and miss, for a while, but they're rebuilding. They need to find the black coven and take care of them. From what the local alpha Tamsin said, the group started killing not only the local witches with a magic infused concoction, they are killing humans as well."

"Fuck. No way. Humans? That's awful flashy of them." Ziry sipped her coffee. She felt like she was listening to a fictional story. "Are people still dying?"

Dad shrugged. "I don't know the full story, but I think they've found a counter-compound. It took the wolves working with the local witches to figure it all out. I guess they have an investigator, but they want a second detective.”

“And you want me to go out there and help?” Excitement surged though her at the thought of something so large to work on.

Mom scoffed. “What, think it’s too hard?”

“Nope, just excited to get away from all this damn snow.”

Chapter 8 - Shop Therapy
Rho

Sage was already at the café when Rho showed up. Just over half the tables were occupied by people enjoying drinks and food, some alone with books or computers, others with a companion or two. The scent of coffee drifted past her making her crave a mug. It was a larger establishment that reviews said made great food.

At a side table, near the windows overlooking a small garden, Sage stood and waved. Her sandy blond hair cascaded in perfect curls down her back and swayed as if in a breeze. A wide smile welcomed Rho and her hazel eyes twinkled in the overhead lights. It always amused Rho how Sage dressed similarly to Cinthia, a loose flowing blouse over a hobo skirt and she wore a patchwork belt with baubles hanging from it.

Think friendly thoughts, Rho. Remember when you were partnered with Brooke in science class? She was the school bitch, but you worked hard to make that experience pleasant ... well, not heinous. You can do this. She straightened and forced herself to look excited ... or at least glad to see Sage.

Rho walked up to her target, and Sage gave her a hug. Her first reaction was to tense up, but a deep breath helped her relax and she hugged the black witch back. This was what she was here for. "I'm so happy you invited me. I was surprised, but this will be fun."

They sat and Rho looked through the menu. "Wow, they have everything."

"Yeah, this place is pretty great." Sage agreed.

When the server, a young man in jeans and a tie-dyed shirt, came over, she ordered a chicken sandwich, a side salad, and a cappuccino. His floppy brown hair and beacher vibe matched the overall ambiance of the place. "Great choice, the cook is famous for his chicken."

Rho sipped her water and smiled at Sage. "I feel awful that I don't know much about you. Where did you come from before coming to Santa Cruz? Were you part of a coven? Was it big? Was there a werewolf pack nearby? Were there issues? Is that why you don't like the pack?" As she spoke, Rho leaned forward, showing her interest.

None of the tables near them were occupied. There was enough of a buzz in the air from other conversations, so Rho wasn't worried about them being overheard.

Sage threw up her hands, shaking them back and forth. "Whoa, slow down there, too fast. Okay, let me see if I can catch all of your questions." She laughed. "I come from a small town in Texas, called Spicewood. It's just a bit northwest of Austin. No one's heard of it. There are witches there, so when I got here, I knew what was going on, but damn, Cinthia has things on lock down."

The waiter dropped off food as Rho gaped, shocked, *Sage is from Texas too? What a small world.* "Spicewood? I think I've heard of it. I can't believe we come from the same neck of the woods and we never discussed it before. I'm from San Marcos, like, an hour or two away. We're practically neighbors."

Sage's eyes widened. "Shut the front door! That's fantastic. How did we never know we were both from Texas?"

"Too much going on, I guess." Rho's head was about to explode. Did this mean there was a group of black witches in Texas, or had they all come to California to take over? *I have to contact my parents and let them know.* She clenched her jaw, then forced a smile to hide her stress. "How is your burger?"

Sage wiped her mouth with a napkin. "Good, good." She took a sip of her soda. "So, to answer your other questions, if you're from the area, then you know that there's a pack, just not that close. Thank the goddess. For the most part, I don't love werewolves." She wrinkled her nose. "Because they stink."

Confusion swamped Rho. "Wait, what? I thought your proficiencies were in fire and plants, like Cinthia. I have an animal proficiency and I can only distinguish a wolf from a human if I really concentrate—and even then it's hit or miss."

Sage shook her head and then bit her lower lip. "No, it's psychosomatic, I'm sure." Rho didn't think it sounded that way but didn't want to upset the tender beginning of this pretend friendship. "My grandparents were part of the early war against the werewolves. They brought up my parents, who then brought me up to be anti-wolf." She sighed. "It's hard to shift from my upbringing."

Gah! I wish I had a werewolf's ability to smell a lie. I'm guessing there isn't a lick of truth in what she just spouted. But once again, Rho pasted on a pleasant face. "Oh! Yeah, that makes sense." She took a bite of her chicken sandwich. "This is really good."

"I know, right! So good." They continued to eat for a few more minutes, then Sage asked, "So, you told me about this pig outfit. Any other shopping?"

"Yes, just some general clothing for high-end parties." She rolled her eyes. "Oh, the glamorous life of a personal shopper."

"I don't know, sounds interesting, you know, if you like shopping all the time. I'm more of a casual purchaser, if you know what I mean." Sage looked off to the distance for a moment. "How are you enjoying everything in Santa Cruz since you've arrived? It's been a lot this last year, right? The wolves have had their ups and down, and then Blake, a wolf and a witch, and now with all the deaths. It's downright like the wild west."

Rho huffed out a laugh. Caroline wasn't out to the entire coven yet about being a wolf. She wondered if Sage knew. *If she doesn't, I'm not going to be the one to tell her, but if she can smell them ... is it possible? No, I'm sure what she said was all, black witches can't sense wolves, that would be ridiculous.* "We're from Texas, known for being rough country, yet I had to come to Santa Cruz for all this crazy. But, to answer your questions, I've liked living here, but I think my client is moving in the next year, and I don't know if I'll fight it."

Sage's eyes widened. "You'll leave the coven?"

"I don't know." Rho shrugged. "I really like everyone, but sometimes I feel, gods, I don't know, stifled. Maybe I shouldn't speak badly of anything with you; you seem really very pro-everything Cinthia and the coven. I'm sorry if I'm putting you in a bad place. I'll stop."

"No, it's fine. I get what you're saying." Sage leaned in and lowered her voice. "I sometimes feel that way too. It's why I've missed some of the weekend meetings. I just need, you know, space."

Rho nodded. *Okay, time to get in with this evil. Time to play the part.* "Exactly. Just a bit of time off once in a while." She slapped her hands over her mouth. "Again, sorry. I don't know what I'm saying."

Sage laughed. "I have a feeling this is the beginning of a beautiful friendship. It looks like you're done. We pay up front. Let's shop."

Chapter 9 - A Whole New World
Ziry

When Ziry was in her twenties—just after she'd graduated college—she'd spent a month of each summer with the different packs across the States. Not every child of the alphas had the opportunity, but her parents wanted her to see how the different wolves ran their packs. Because of this, she knew most of the alphas and many of the wolves in the U.S. When she learned that the South Carolina pack had been destroyed, she'd lit a fire and spent time memorializing each wolf.

She remembered Tamsin ... sort of. She'd visited Santa Cruz probably fifteen years ago, when she was twenty-four and Tamsin was fourteen. The summer before high school, she was never around; always out with friends or other pack members, getting into trouble.

After her tour all those years ago, Ziry mostly stayed in South Dakota. She loved her pack, her family, and their land. She never felt a need to leave. Sitting in the center seat on the plane, she wanted to snarl ... not at the other passengers, but at her brother who'd made the reservations. He'd done it on purpose. Once she landed, she made sure he knew the consequences of not fixing her return flight reservation.

Dad had told her to look for a Subaru Solterra outside the airport. Along the curb, she found a row of dozens of cars. She started walking down the sidewalk when a beautiful brunette halfway down the line waved. "Ziry! Over here. My gods, you look exactly the same."

She smiled and made her way to Tamsin. The trunk was open, and she placed her bags inside. A second woman sat in the passenger seat, so she scooted into the back seat. *This is their territory, their domain, there is no disrespect sitting in the back.* "Thanks. I wasn't sure how long it would take to find you."

The interior of the car was comfortable, and she could smell the scents of different wolves ... and witches. There wasn't a large witch coven in South Dakota, so the idea of there being enough of them to ride share with the pack's alpha was intriguing.

Tamsin pulled out into traffic. "Not a problem. I'm glad you could make it." She merged then smiled at Ziry in the rear view mirror. "Meet Paige. She's my partner."

The woman in the passenger seat turned to look at Ziry. "Hi, nice to meet you." The fact that she was a submissive wolf helped Ziry to relax.

"Nice to meet you as well. Have you been part of the pack for very long?"

"No, my one year wolfy anniversary is coming up in a couple of months." Her eyes danced with amusement.

"Oh, did you cross over to the dark side to be with Tamsin?" Ziry waggled her eyebrows suggestively. She hadn't changed any wolves and knew it wasn't romantic, but she couldn't fathom anyone but the alpha biting this beauty.

The emotions that flashed across Paige's face were too fast for Ziry to read. *Hmm, a story.* She perked up at something to learn outside of the black witches she came to find. Finally, Paige shook her head. "No, that's a longer story, and you're here for our black witches. Maybe after we get you caught up on *that* story we can backtrack to awful alphas who attack innocent bystanders."

"Please tell me you weren't changed against your will." A low growl bubbled up from her gut. It sounded like there were out-of-control wolves who needed dealing with. Or, by the relaxed postures of Tamsin and Paige, maybe Tamsin had already cleaned house.

"Okay!" Paige said in an overly chipper voice. "I won't tell you."

Ziry slumped. "Did you at least know about werewolves before the attack?"

"Nope."

Ziry's lip twitched up in a sneer. "I now understand Tamsin's decision to finally take back her family's pack."

Tamsin chuckled. "Look at you go. No wonder you're an investigator."

"Detective," Ziry corrected.

"Oh, I'm sorry. The person already working on the case is a private investigator. It's just the term I've been using. Anyway, thank you so much for coming. I have a room at pack house. Let me know what you need, and I'll answer any questions you have."

I wonder if this other person is any good. Will they get in my way? Slow me down? I usually work alone. Gah, well, I guess working with someone else will be another lesson to add to my alpha training. Go, me!

Ziry yawned. It wasn't late but travel always took a lot out of her. "I want to know everything. How did this all start? What am I dealing with? How did black witches end up in Santa Cruz? Do you have any files, paperwork, or electronic details started?"

They spent a few minutes discussing heart attacks and black witches. Ziry was shocked at how brazen the black witches had been. She pushed her exhaustion to the side—she could deal with that later, she had a job to do.

"Okay, I want to meet the investigator as soon as possible. I need to determine what each of us should focus on. I'd also like to meet Caroline and Mazzy ... and, well, others."

They'd finally made it from the airport to town and were navigating residential streets. Tamsin turned her Solterra into the driveway of a manor-sized house and then inside a huge garage. "You'll meet anyone and everyone. We can arrange a get-together with you and Rho tomorrow. We'll give you her contact information." She swung into a spot and turned off the car. "Welcome home!"

Chapter 10 - Welcome to My Office
Rho

The smells of the ocean, slightly salty with the briny scent of seaweed and fish, washed over Rho as she sat on the beach. She curled her toes in the sand, the cool breeze sending chills down her spine. Ever since moving to

California, sitting by the ocean was one of her favorite places to be.

Late Sunday afternoon, Tamsin sent her contact information for a person named Ziry. Shortly afterward, Ziry texted her asking where they could touch base. Rho requested the beach. It was a fairly private place where they could talk without being easily seen or overheard. It was also peaceful, and she loved being there. If the person ended up being an ass, at least she could enjoy the view of the water.

She sent a digital map link to where she wanted to meet and hoped Ziry could find her. Until then, she enjoyed the peace that came with watching the ocean washing in and out.

"Is this seat taken?"

Rho looked over her shoulder and her breath caught. Standing above her was a stunning woman with long, wavy, dark auburn hair that reached her mid-back. Pale green eyes, the color of moss that grew on the sides of trees, twinkled in the sunlight. She wore a flowing, pale blue, see-through wrap over a navy blue bikini with cherries on it.

Gah! I want to lick those cherries. She blushed at her thought and turned back to watch the waves.

Rho shook her head. *Where did that thought come from?* She took a calming breath, trying to slow her pounding heart. "Depends, the beach is free for anyone, but I am waiting for someone." She gazed back at the beauty. "You don't happen to be Ziry, do you?"

The woman smiled, and Rho tried not to swoon. She quickly turned to look out over the ocean again. She had to get control over herself.

The air moved as the woman sat down next to her. "I assume you're Rho. It's nice to meet you."

In her peripheral vision, Rho saw a hand. She reached out and shook. Tingles tickled her to her toes. "Nice to meet you as well." *Gods above, I hope I'm the only one feeling this ... or maybe I shouldn't hope that. What does she think of a casual fling?*

"Is Rho short for something?" Ziry asked, her smile like a beacon to a lost moth.

Before she could censor herself, Rho did the one thing she never did, she told the truth. "Yeah, it's short for Rhonda. Heh, my parents ... what can ya do?"

Ziry chuckled. "Is that why you're a detective? 'Help me Rhonda, help, help me Rhonda.'" She sang the lyrics and the spell broke.

Rho groaned. "How about you forget I told you my real name, and I never hear that song from your lips again." Her focus dropped to the luscious mouth when she'd mentioned the lips, and she quickly shut her eyes. *I need to get a grip or working with this person will become an issue. I'm in my thirties, what the hell? I'm acting like a horny teen!*

"Okay, no Beach Boys, got it." Rho opened her eyes again and saw Ziry leaning back on her hands, gazing out over the water. "It's amazing out here. Not many people in the water. I thought it would be swimmers all day."

Rho laughed. "I know you're from South Dakota, but they do have the internet there, right? This isn't really the part of the ocean where people swim year round. You can swim, it'll be warmer than where you came from, but trust me, it's chilly."

"So, the ocean in winter is more a spectator sport?"

"Exactly."

Ziry nodded. "Well, this is better than the snowy tundra I just came from. Though, I do love the four seasons."

"I come from Texas, so this is already cold for me. Maybe one day I'll live with snow, but I've never sought that lifestyle out."

They sat for a few moments, enjoying the beach and the calming effect of the ocean. Rho spent the time reminding herself why they were there. This was about the black witches, not cherries.

Finally, Ziry sat up. "Okay, let's discuss this case and what's going on. I hear you have a plan."

"I do. How much do you know?"

"I think I'm fully caught up. Tamsin and Paige were pretty thorough on the way in from the airport."

With the calm from the beach, Rho finally could focus again. "Okay, well, I'm starting to gain Sage's trust. We have some odd similarities besides both being fairly new witches to the area. I'm hoping to continue to become best buds with her. If I can get to where she opens up to me, that would be perfect."

Ziry nodded. "So, I assume you're showing her how much the coven is annoying you, bristling with its rules and all that?"

"Something like that."

"Okay, so you're working on the one known black witch; that leaves me with the other one. The nurse that worked with Tory. She's still in custody. High security since the other one ended up dead." Ziry's gaze shifted up to the clouds, large and fluffy in the sky. "Mildred, one of the wolves, can get me Nia's address. I'll start there. I know the police already searched her place, but I may be able to find out more."

Rho smiled. "Okay, you take Nia, I have Sage. It sounds like we have our marching orders."

"When should we meet next?"

"Well, you just got here. I'm guessing it will take some time to find your way around. I also don't have any plans with Sage until next week. Maybe next weekend? Unless something comes up. Say, Saturday afternoon?"

"Sounds great, we can meet here. Unless you want to go somewhere else?" Did she sound hopeful?

"No, this is private. It works for these meetings." *Unless you want to go out to dinner, dancing, and something more? Are you up for more, wolf?*

Ziry made a noncommittal sound. "Until then." As she walked away, Rho admired that view as much as she had appreciated the front.

For fuck's sake, I need to get control of myself!

Chapter 11 - What's A Little Breaking and Entering Amongst Friends
Ziry

A chill worked its way down Ziry's back. *I can't believe how chilly it is. Aren't I in California?*

She wrapped her hands around her coffee and drank deeply of the delicious brew. She'd woken up at her normal time, well before most of the others in pack house, and caught a ride to The Daily Grind with Bexlee, who stopped on her way to the precinct.

She had a tablet with notes. Over the week she'd been in town, she'd rented a car, gotten Nia's address from Mildred, learned how to get from pack house to Nia's apartment, and made a plan. It was Wednesday, and after watching the apartment building for a few days, she knew she could slip in at eleven after one of the neighbors left to take their dog for a daily walk. The woman always left from the back door, which had a stronger lock, but wasn't being monitored by the police.

The three days Ziry watched the apartment, she saw a variety of people in the front and back. No one seemed to know each other, just blank but friendly nods.

She double-checked her outfit, a cream suit with a russet button-down shirt. She had a large purse containing her lock picking set, a flashlight, a pad of paper, pen, gloves, and other odds and ends she may need for the day. The purse had the benefit of being able to fit anything she found.

Along with the outfit, she appeared like any professional woman.

Once she'd double-checked everything, she walked the couple of blocks back to the pack house and got into her car. She drove to Nia's place and parked. The police still had people watching the outside of the building. Probably hoping to find any connections to Nia and the creators of the heart attack concoction. *Get in line.*

Ziry parked a block away and walked up to the complex with determination. Two buildings away, she opened her purse, which hung from her arm, and started searching through it, as if looking for her keys. She turned on the walkway that led to the back, as she'd seen a dozen other people who lived there do.

As she reached the backyard, the door opened, and a young woman came out with a large dog. Ziry grasped the door to help the other woman slip out more easily. She smiled and mumbled a thank you, before being dragged down the path to the sidewalk.

Ziry swung around the door and into Nia's building.

Her heart pounded as she found the stairs and headed up to the fourth floor. Nia's place was unit four-twelve. Thankfully, it was on the back, though Ziry didn't plan on turning on any lights.

At the top of the stairs, the hallway went in both directions. Ziry turned right. The hallway had eight doors, four to the left, four to the right. Everything felt silent and still. *Everyone must be at work or school. Thank the gods.*

Nia's unit was easy to find—the police tape was a dead giveaway. She put on her gloves, pulled out her lock picking kit, and made quick work of getting the door open. Ducking under the yellow strip, she slipped in and shut the door.

The apartment was stifling and dark. It had been empty since Nia's arrest. It smelled stale, though the neighbors had cooked curry recently and another had eaten Chinese food. Ziry replaced the kit in her purse and found her penlight. The first room was a great room: living room, dining room, and kitchen combined.

The area was tidy. There were two doors. One went to a bathroom, the other a bedroom. Ziry started in the bedroom. She did a quick look through the drawers. As she expected, she didn't find anything. The police had already searched, and she didn't think there'd be anything in any place obvious.

After checking the closet, she knocked on each of the walls. She didn't find anything. On the shelf, there were stacks of folded clothes but nothing else. Hanging on a hook was a purse. In it was a set of keys. The purse was small and had a few other items in it. She put the full sack in her larger bag. *Maybe one of the keys is an apartment key. If I need to return, it would be much easier.*

Ziry slid her hand between the mattress and the box spring. When she didn't find anything, she went to the foot of the bed and lifted it up. In the center was a travel purse usually worn around one's neck. Ziry grabbed it, let the mattress down, and put the bag in her purse.

Next she checked out the bathroom. Again she didn't expect to find anything much. The drawers were full of makeup and other toiletries. She lifted the lid of the toilet tank. Floating in the water was a sealed plastic bag. In the kitchen, Ziry found tongs, a small towel, and a plastic bag. Back in the bathroom she fished out the loot, dried it off, put everything in the bag, and put it in her purse for later investigation.

The only other place that looked like it had any promise was a desk in the living room. It took a quarter-hour of tapping and lightly rubbing tops and bottoms of drawers, but Ziry found a hidden compartment. Papers, a thumb drive, a small notebook, pens, and a few other odds and ends. She emptied everything from it into her purse.

With a final look, Ziry decided she'd found what she could ... at least for now. She could always come back.

At the door, she shut her eyes and listened.

"I heard this door shut, Howard."

"No, you didn't. It's been closed since the cops put up the tape. You're just imagining things."

"I'm going to go tell those boys in the car what I heard."

"You do that."

"I'm going to bring some cookies, too."

"You do that, Bertha, I'm sure they'll appreciate it."

"You keep watch."

"Oh, I will. I won't leave this spot."

Ziry's heart sped up. *How am I going to escape if Howard is monitoring the place? Fuck!*

There was a shuffling and a door closed. "I'll be back, Howard."

After a minute, Ziry heard a chuckle. "If you're listening robber, I'm going to the bathroom. Escape now. I'll be back in five ... well, ten minutes. Bertha took the elevator, so take the stairs." He chuckled as she heard footsteps and a door close.

The hallway finally sounded and felt empty. To be certain, she cracked the door open and peeked out ... no one, perfect!

Once she reached the stairs, she forced herself to walk slowly down to the main floor. Outside, she pulled out the keys she'd found and tested them. One turned in the back door, reopening the door. With a sigh of relief and a smirk, she headed back towards her car.

Back at the pack house, she went to her room to investigate her findings. The travel bag was just that. It had a fake id and money— U.S. dollars, pesos, Canadian dollars, and euros. A go-bag.

After opening the plastic bag full of stuff from the toilet tank, Ziry threw away the tongs and towel.

In the sealed bag was a cell phone. Though she could turn it on, it was locked. *I wonder if anyone here can hack into this and pull information from it.* She set it aside.

Lastly, she sorted through the papers and items from the concealed desk compartment. There were three vials. She'd have to give them to Mazzy for testing. On the papers was information about different building sites. Locations around Santa Cruz with costs to rent or buy. Phone numbers with names of owners and realtors.

Each property had information on whether it would work as a lab. Specs on open rooms, ventilation for mixing chemicals, and if there was a space for cold storage.

Excitement surged through her. Ziry's search had dropped from the city to half a dozen locations.

Her part of the job was going well. *I wonder how that sexy brunette is doing with befriending the enemy? She's gorgeous, which makes working with her better from afar. I'd rather work alone, but if we have to work side by side, I won't be responsible for my actions ... assuming she's game for side activities. I wonder if she has skills to match her looks, gah, she'd be the full package, save being a witch who lives in California! I have to stop thinking about her!*

Chapter 12 - Sage Advice
Rho

It had been two weeks since Rho had gone shopping for a pig outfit with Sage. They'd texted a few times, but hadn't found a time to get together until Friday night for dinner. They'd decided on an Italian restaurant. It was casual dining, most of the other tables were filled with families and kids. A few other tables had couples, which is what they looked to be.

Once they were seated, they took a few minutes to decide on what they wanted to eat. Sage chose lasagna while Rho went for chicken parmesan. They both asked for glasses of red wine.

"How was your week?" Sage sipped her wine as they waited for their food to come.

"It was good. Veronica loved the outfit. She said it went over well at the event last weekend. What about yours?"

"Eh, I spend my days running the books at a used car lot. It's boring. Nothing to tell you about my days." She wrinkled her nose, then raised her glass for another sip.

"You sell cars for a living? No wonder you're such a fast talker!"

Sage guffawed. "I wish. I'd rather be out on the lot, but no, I get the customers once they've picked out a new set of wheels. They sit with me, and I have to explain the numbers to them. Step by step I work through the paperwork with them. It's a thrill a minute. Nothing like a pig-couture."

Rho laughed. "That was something, wasn't it? I hear the weekend went well."

"What? No pictures?" Sage put on a mock-offended face.

Smiling wide, Rho pulled out her phone and found her text exchange for the night of the event. Veronica had sent a slew of images of all the people, including herself.

Rho and Sage had found a pink pair of biker shorts and matching bikini top. They paired it with a tulle skirt. Lastly, they found pig ears and a tail that Veronica could wiggle on command.

Veronica had worn her hair down and the dark waves came just past her shoulders. Her bright blue eyes sparkled in every shot. She'd taken selfies with just about every celebrity, and wanna-be celebrity at the event.

Sage scooted her chair around, and they pointed and laughed over the different costumes, each more outlandish than the last.

"Look at that one, we should've bought her a mask. It's so classy!" Sage shook her head in amusement.

"Did you just call one of these outfits ... classy?"

"Well, the cause is classy if nothing else."

Rho sighed. "That's true."

"Are you saying you wouldn't have gone if invited?"

"It was during a coven event. Even if I *had* been invited, you know I'd have had to make some sort of excuse." Rho rolled her eyes and slumped in her seat.

The server chose that moment to bring their food. Once the server left, Sage tilted her head. "Are you feeling stifled by the demands of the coven?"

Rho swallowed the bite of food she'd taken. "No, of course not. I love the coven and my sisters."

A soft smile warmed Sage's face. "You know you can talk to me, right? I'm a safe person. Here, I'll tell you a truth, and then you can tell me a truth."

Leaning back, Rho gazed at Sage for a moment before finally nodding in agreement.

Sage's smile widened. "Okay, here it is. I know we're friends with the wolves, but like I told you last time, they make me uncomfortable. I keep trying to get over my parents' bias, but I just can't. I wish we were less of a united front, and more two separate groups."

Rho let the information sink in. She knew that about Sage, but probably not everyone else did.

Thinking about it, she realized she could tell the black witch a partial truth. "Okay, yes, I sometimes feel stifled by the coven." She waved her hands as if to stop what she'd just said. "I do love the others in the coven, but I'm used to having more freedom ... you know."

In reality, though she loved to move around, this was the first time she'd felt at home with a coven. She could see planting roots in Santa Cruz. They were anything but stifling.

"I do. I totally get what you're saying. And don't worry about telling me. We're friends ... sisters, right?" Sage leaned forward and started to reach out her hands, as if she wanted to connect physically.

Rho's shoulders dropped. "Right. Yes, sisters." She forced a smile.

"You okay?"

"I am, I just ... it feels weird talking about this with anyone. I haven't even told my family how I feel, and I used to be close with them. I would tell them everything."

Sage finally reached over and took her hand, giving it a squeeze. "Just remember, you have me, and you can tell me anything. I'm safe."

Rho squeezed her hand back, resisting the urge to slip her hand away. *Nope, not safe at all, but we can pretend. Imagine you're holding that sexy wolf's hand. What if you were out to dinner with her?* Suddenly her whole body relaxed and she smiled wide.

Chapter 13 - A Proposition
Ziry

It had been two weeks since Ziry's alphas, her parents, had given her the assignment to come to Santa Cruz and help the Pacific Pack deal with the influx of black witches. Two days after that discussion, she'd walked onto this beach for the first time and met the devastatingly beautiful witch she was supposed to partner with. Her only hope was to avoid the woman. Not only was she not a wolf, she was a witch, and lived thousands of miles from her home in South Dakota.

As she made her way across the sand, she saw Rho with her short bob haircut, the loose locks blowing in the wind. The sunshine highlighted skin of a bronze. Like last time she wore dark blue linen pants and a light, short sleeve, moss-colored sweater.

Ziry stopped beside her and wanted to growl in approval. Even her herbal witch smell dug deep into her soul, calling to her. It'd been several months ... *had it been longer?* ... since she'd been so taken by someone else. "I see you've reserved my spot again."

Dark eyes, the color of her hair, gazed over her shoulder. Ziry wanted to imagine she smelled the other woman's desire but wasn't sure if it was Rho's or her own she sensed. Rho smiled. "I guess I did. Have any luck over the last two weeks?"

Sitting on the sand, Ziry stretched her legs out towards the water. Unlike last time, she wore jeans and a T-shirt. She'd learned her lesson about the beach. She leaned back on her hands and watched the waves in the distance. "I did. After getting Nia's address, I staked it out, then broke in."

Rho leaned over and tapped her shoulder to Ziry's. A jolt of sensation shot through Ziry, and she shivered. Rho said, "Find anything interesting. Was it worth it?"

Ziry dug her fingers into the sand and took a stabilizing breath. She hoped the other woman didn't notice. "I found a few locations of where the lab could be. I thought it was all pretty straightforward, but she wrote in code. I've been working to decipher it and find the buildings. There are four possible locations after I eliminated two. Once we find the place, I'll form a strike-team with some of the wolves, go in, and tear the place down."

"Gods, I'd love to be part of all that." Rho's arm rubbed against hers again. *Is this all chance, or is the beauty flirting with me? Gods, I wish I were better at this.* Rho continued. "I'm guessing your team won't include witches, though you know, we can be rather useful."

Trying to focus on their conversation and the calming ocean, Ziry nodded. "True, but your job will be to keep Sage occupied. We don't want her showing up at the lab and giving us more friction."

Rho's head fell back. "Well, at least I get to do something." She straightened up. "But you don't have a timeline yet?"

"Not until we find the place. We can't put together a plan until we know where we're going."

"That makes sense." Rho slowly nodded as she looked off into the distance.

A comfortable silence fell over them for a few moments before Ziry asked, "What about you? How has your plan been going?"

Rho smiled and Ziry's heart skipped a beat. "Good. Sage is setting herself up as my one true friend. The only person I can truly open up to. She's getting me to admit how overbearing the coven is."

Ziry chuckled. "That's great. It sounds like you have things well handled. What's the next step there?"

With a grunt, Rho faced Ziry and screwed her face up into a scowl. "More socializing with her. She's nice, but I feel like I need to shower every time I leave."

Ziry's cheeks hurt from her smile. *When was the last time I smiled this much? I'm having fun.* "Sounds awful."

Rho rolled her eyes. "Yeah. I can feel your sympathy." The deadpan was perfect.

They both chuckled before another silence fell. It was comfortable and they both watched the waves as they crashed on the shore. There were a few other people scattered around, but it was a pleasant and uncrowded time to sit and enjoy the beach. *I could really get used to this.*

"Hey, beautiful, want a free surfing lesson?"

Ziry looked up to see a tall, fit man stood over them, blocking the sun. Rho scooted closer to her.

The man's brows came together. "Oh, I'm sorry. Are the two of you on a date?"

Ziry said, "No," at the same time Rho mumbled, "I'm trying but some people are just impossible."

The man laughed, having obviously heard her words. He shook his head and walked away.

Ziry turned to Rho. "What did you say?" She had excellent hearing. She'd heard the witch but hadn't expected anything like that. Her heart pounded and she worked to keep a blank face.

"Well, I mean, I'm sorry if you're not into women, but you're only here for a few weeks ... and gorgeous, and, well, if you're not interested in a fling, no worries." She sounded so ... blasé.

Throwing caution to the wind, Ziry reached over and gave into several fantasies she'd had since meeting Rho. Tilting up the other woman's chin, she gently kissed her.

Chapter 14 - Dinner and Dessert
Rho

Did I really say that? Rho kept a smile plastered on her face as she watched Ziry's reaction to her words. *What if Ziry only likes men? What if she likes women, but not witches? What if she just doesn't find me attractive?*

Finally, Ziry smiled back, reached over to tilt up her chin, and kissed her. An explosion of sensations went off in Rho's body and it took everything she had not to pounce.

"You know, you're right. I'm only here for a short amount of time, I guess getting whatever this is—" she waved her hand between them, "—out of my ... our systems, would be a good idea."

Relief flooded Rho. She'd debated laughing and taking it all back but knew werewolves could hear lies. Ziry would know the truth of her first statement. In the end, she knew she had to wait the other woman out.

Rho licked her dry lips, trying to maintain her confidence. "Well, I know we're trying to keep things on the down low. If you want, I could make you salmon and vegetables for dinner. It isn't much, but it's what I have in my fridge."

Ziry smiled. "That sounds amazing. I have it on good authority that finding someone who can cook fish is well worth the endeavor."

Rho gave Ziry directions to her apartment, and they drove separately. She left the beach area first, and Ziry agreed to give her a ten to fifteen minute head start. That would help to ensure no one who shouldn't would see them together.

Once home, she did a quick walk-through to make sure it looked neat and tidy. Then she started pulling ingredients from the refrigerator. Ziry showed up a few minutes later with a lemon cheesecake.

"I wasn't sure if you had anything for dessert, so I picked something up on the way."

Taking the box, Rho smiled. "This looks great."

Rho directed the other woman to the small table that had two chairs, and she went back into the kitchen and started cooking.

"Do you need any help?"

There were two skillets on the stove, one where the zucchini sauteed, the other had the salmon. She had a pot with some asparagus steaming. Rho pointed to a cabinet. "There are plates in there." She pointed down. "Silverware is in there. If you want to set the table?"

Rho went back to what she was doing. The fish was ready to come out of the skillet. She placed it on a platter. Her timer for the asparagus went off, and that went onto another plate with the zucchini. She brought it all over to the table. She loved cooking for friends, and she felt this was something more. *No, not more, just a fling.*

Ziry smiled. "This all looks fantastic! I'm impressed you can cook."

A warmth filled Rho, but she just shrugged. "It's nothing."

They ate in silence for a few minutes. Rho asked, "Are you adjusting to the no snow?"

A smile flashed across Ziry's face for a moment. "You know, landing here was strange. Stuffing away my winter coat, gloves, scarf, the works. But in the end, I swear your homes are chillier than mine back home. Ours have better insulation from the temperature change. I wake up here and the chill is deep in my bones. Now, outside it's lovely."

"The older homes are drafty, but this apartment is relatively new. You should be comfortable here. Nice and warm."

Ziry lifted her wine glass in salute. "This doesn't hurt."

Once they'd finished, Rho cleared away the dishes and sliced two pieces of cheesecake. "We could eat here or take it into the living room and turn on a movie."

"A movie sounds great. I love the idea of relaxing ... having some down time."

After some debating, they ended up on *Alien.* Ziry made an approving sound. "Any movie where the woman is the only smart one and she saves the cat ... classic."

They both sat on the couch, and Rho put her cheesecake on the table after taking a bite. "That's amazing. Have you ever made one yourself?"

Ziry laughed. "Don't get me wrong, I'm not a terror in the kitchen, but yes, I tried to make cheesecake once. I think I added too much milk, or cream, or ... I don't know. It didn't set. When I removed the sides of the baking dish, liquid goo flowed over the island, onto the floor, and everywhere. Both my brothers were there, and, well, I've avoided most kitchen duty ever since."

Rho chuckled. "Does your pack have a rotation?"

"Yeah. My dad loves to cook. He usually wakes up early and makes food for any early birds. Others take over later on the weekends. During the week, after about eight in the morning, everyone is on their own. Dad is close to retirement but loves his job and hasn't lost steam yet."

Their legs brushed and chills chased each other through Rho's body. She tried to hide a tremble as she slid a bit closer.

Rho leaned back on the couch and got the movie started. As the first scenes played, Ziry placed her hand on Rho's leg, and Rho had to focus on her breathing to hide how much it affected her.

As the movie continued, Ziry's hand moved up to Rho's thigh. She concentrated so much on the hand and its path that when Ziry tightened her grip and tensed, Rho realized she had no idea where they were in the movie.

Ziry gaze shifted to her. "Wow, you're made of stern stuff, you didn't even flinch at that."

Rho felt her face heat. "I may have been focusing on other things."

Ziry shifted so she better faced Rho, then smirked. "Oh, I can help with that." Moving slowly, she leaned in, cupping the back of Rho's head with her free hand.

The kiss started soft. Rho's heart pounded fast, and she leaned in, enjoying the feel of Ziry's commanding mouth. A warm tongue traced her lips, and she inhaled in shock as the electricity between them intensified. Ziry took the invitation to deepen the kiss, and Rho lost herself in the taste of tart lemon and something darker that was all the sexy wolf.

Sliding her hands over to Ziry, Rho let her exploration go from legs to waist. Ziry's shirt was untucked, and the velvety soft skin underneath invited touch. It didn't take long for Rho to discover Ziry didn't wear a bra, and she groaned as she let herself spend time exploring the perfect curves of the other woman's breasts.

Her thumbs rubbed over the taught nubs of Ziry's nipples, and she moaned into Rho's mouth. Shivers of lust trembled through her as she stroked each lovely mound, enjoying the sensations.

The sound of a zipper and the feel of a hand on her lower abdomen let her know Ziry's next destination. The woman quickly unfastened Rho's pants, then her nimble fingers were down her panties and ... oh, gods! Rho froze as her world became the zings of sensation from the hand on her breast and the thumb on her clit. She quivered with need.

Pushing forward, Ziry maneuvered Rho until she lay on the couch beneath her. The pressure intensified, and Rho moved her hips with Ziry's motions. She was so close. She panted, lifting her hips, wanting, needing, silently begging.

Ziry reached down to pull off Rho's clothes, then went back to playing with her most sensitive areas. With her other hand, she slid a finger, then two, into Rho, gliding in and out.

Rho thrashed on the couch, not caring about the sounds she made. She was so close. Gods above, this woman!

Ziry's voice flowed over her, low and husky. "That's it, come for me. Scream. I want to hear your orgasm, then taste it on my fingers."

Rho gasped at the words, then her world fractured. Ziry continued to play, extending the pleasure for as long as Rho could take it.

Once she began to whimper, Ziry stopped, pulled out her fingers, and then licked them off. "Mmm, you taste delicious."

Rho smiled, though she barely had any energy. "I can't wait to see how you taste, wolf."

Chapter 15 - Moon Dance
Tamsin

The drive from campus to pack house was busier than normal, and Tamsin wanted to strangle the steering wheel. Her jaw clenched and she blew her horn at a silver Audi that cut her off. *Isn't it enough that I have to deal with* *teenagers? Do I also have to fight traffic every day as well?*

All she wanted to do when she got home was hide in the alpha suite. As she pulled into the garage and saw one of the construction vehicles, she remembered she and Paige were stuck in the tiniest of rooms until the bathroom was redone. *For fuck's sake, it better be worth it!*

She knew it would be, but on days like this, she debated the rationale of redoing the bathroom and the decision to not get a hotel room for the duration. *If Georgette spearheaded the brigade to not let me leave for Colorado for the research mission, I doubt the pack would be any happier if Paige and I were hunkered down under a different roof.*

Tamsin parked and sat in the car, fingers digging into the abused steering wheel, trying to get her body to relax.

The day wasn't that bad. Just a few uppity students. A meeting with the chair and a few professors to discuss how she could improve. Everyone was evaluated; it was nothing to worry about. Just another Monday.

Except it wasn't. The pull of the moon distracted her this month. Not to mention, she hated when the full moon fell during the school week, especially on a Monday. She wanted to be with her pack and nowhere else. For some reason, the pull was especially strong this month, and she itched to be with her own, even in her human skin. But she craved to be running on four paws.

After a few more calming breaths, she got out of the car and entered the house. She headed up the backstairs to the room she and Paige were sharing. She tossed her bag on the desk and collapsed onto the bed. At the door, Paige snorted. She must have heard Tamsin come in and followed close behind.

"Rough day?"

"As lovely as the moon's song is to my soul, it makes the students loony. Add to that my review, and you have a recipe for my missing you all day long."

Paige sashayed over and climbed onto the bed, straddling Tamsin. "You know, you almost always claim you miss me. I think you're just trying to figure out the right words to get me out of my clothes."

"Well, are any of them working?"

She laughed, leaned down, and kissed Tamsin. The magic of her beautiful mate worked, and Tamsin finally started to relax. After pushing back up, Paige gazed down into Tamsin's eyes. "Better?"

"Yeah, though us having the rest of the night to ourselves would be even better."

"Bullshit. You love full moon nights and running with the pack. Not to mention, Connie, chef extraordinaire, is making Greek food tonight. I guess she had some the other day and has a craving." Paige stroked Tamsin's hair, helping her to relax more.

Tamsin pushed herself up, coming face to face with the other woman, and smiled mischievously. "So, that's the trick. Feed her the food you want her to cook a few days before the full moon. Get her thinking about it, and then she'll make it for us?"

Paige returned Tamsin's grin. "We'll have to test this theory, it has merit."

They headed down and found Georgette, Maria, and Blake in the living room. The smells from the kitchen made Tamsin's belly grumble. Before she sat, she yelled, "Need help cooking?" The voices of other pack members and the clatter of utensils, pots, and pans told Tamsin the room wasn't wanting for help, but she wanted to make sure to offer.

Connie popped her head out of the opening to the kitchen. "Nah, I have a few people in here. One more and the kitchen may explode. Sit, rest. You cook enough around here." She disappeared as fast as she had appeared.

Paige linked her arm in Tamsin's and pulled her to the love seat.

Maria smiled as they sat. "We were kicked out of there as well. So, two more months until the big wedding. Have you changed your mind yet? Decided to follow in our footsteps and elope?"

"Gods, I wish," Tamsin mumbled while Paige laughed and said, "Of course not. The pack is so excited."

Blake shook her head at Tamsin, then faced Paige. "So, have you found dresses yet?"

Tamsin grumbled, but Paige leaned forward, as if sharing state secrets. "We decided to work with one of the witches. Rho."

A smile stretched across Blake's face. "That's perfect. She's really good at her job."

From the other couch, Georgette leaned back, the glint in her eyes warning of trouble. "What I want to know is, once you're married, is one of you going to get pregnant? I want a baby to dote over."

Tamsin rubbed her eyes. It was the one question she and Paige hadn't really discussed. She knew they should, but things had just ... happened.

Next to her, Paige stroked her back. "I don't know about Tam, but not right away. I'd like to be married for a bit and enjoy our new territory. But give us our bliss, and maybe. I think raising a baby or two would be pretty great ... if we can find a good donor."

Maria raised her hand. "I'll take her answer."

"Aren't you a bit old to be copying off someone else's paper?" Georgette snorted.

"Not when it was such a good answer." Maria shrugged.

The conversation was interrupted by dinner. The scents brought everyone to the dining room. The house was packed, which brought joy to Tamsin's heart. After they ate, they headed out in sets of twos and threes to run. She and Paige were in the last group.

Running down the trail, Tamsin could smell that the family of cats recently had kittens. She worried one of the dogs who ran the trail daily would find the poor kits.

The eucalyptus was strong and almost covered the scent of wild turkey. At the pack meeting spot, almost two dozen wolves waited, sniffing and investigating the area.

A few yips, and Tamsin had them all together, ready to run. The first part of the night, they'd all need to stretch their muscles and move. The turkeys would have to wait. Yips, barks, and howls followed her as she ran.

After a mile or so, she sensed a few wolves pulling away, starting to head towards an area they avoided because it skirted residential backyards.

Following the connections she had with the pack, she found that Joyce and Orin were drifting. *"Orin, where are you going?"*

She felt him falter. *"I ... I don't know. I'm ... there is a pull. I'm following. I ... I'm sorry. I am back with you."*

She had a similar conversation with Joyce.

Distracted with the rest of the pack and the pull of the moon, Tamsin decided to consider the odd behavior of two of her wolves after the run. For now there was the joy of being the wolf.

They got as far away from the pack house as she wanted to roam. The pack had had a good run and the feel from her wolves was happiness. It brought joy to her heart. Tamsin turned the wolves around and headed back. This time she searched for prey.

She led her group to a flock of wild turkeys. As alpha, she directed the wolves, putting them in groups, keeping them organized. While they descended, finding their marks, dispatching, and feasting, Tamsin took account of each pack member, to make sure no one was hurt.

In one trio, she had Jett, Mazzy, and her newest wolf, Caroline. Bexlee ran with her two dads and Wynn. Maria, Blake, and Georgette went after a turkey together. Then there was Jolly, Timothy, and Toby; Tory, Mildred, and Cyrus; and lastly Connie, Orin, and Joyce, who included Ziry with them.

Paige stayed out with Tamsin. It was a lot to organize, but everyone moved like a well-oiled machine.

Everyone seemed to be working well in their clusters, and Tamsin was about to go after her own turkey, when she realized that Connie was standing alone. Tamsin narrowed her eyes but could see her partners. *"Connie, why are you not with your group?"*

She gazed around the field. *"They ran off. I refused to leave you."*

Tamsin reached out for Orin or Joyce but couldn't find them. She tried again with a snarl and found Joyce. Her mental connection came back weak. *"I don't know what's happening. I just ... I'll return."*

The connection snapped back into place, and Tamsin felt Joyce shake as she rearranged herself before returning.

That left Orin. Tamsin found Georgette and asked her to watch over the pack. Then she headed off in the direction she'd felt Joyce's wispy trail. Once away from the rest of the wolves, she found Orin, Joyce, and Ziry's scents. *What is happening to my wolves? Could this be the black witches? Should I bring more pack with me?*

She picked up her speed to follow them. When Joyce's trail veered away, she dismissed it, focusing on her missing link.

About a mile away, she found Orin and Ziry. They were tracking ... she sniffed the air, a rabbit. Frustration surged through her, she reminded herself Ziry probably didn't know what was going on. *At least I hope not.* She got between the two and lowered herself, snarling at Ziry, baring her teeth in challenge.

Ziry, almost as big as Tamsin, and her wolf a similar red, snarled back. *Fucking alphas. Don't know what's good for them.* Tamsin released the full weight of her alpha power, blanketing the area. She knew Ziry would be the next alpha of her pack, but she wasn't an alpha yet, and earning the spot gave a wolf some privileges.

Both Ziry and Orin whimpered and dropped to their bellies.

Teeth still barred, Tamsin jerked her muzzle towards the pack house, the message clear. *Ziry, your run is done.*

Since Ziry wasn't part of her pack, she couldn't speak with her directly, but the wolf would understand her presence was no longer welcome in their pack run. Ziry's eyes widened, and she whined, but she slunk off with her head lowered. Once she was far enough away to not be disrespectful, she pulled herself up and ran.

Heading back to the others, Tamsin tried to hide her frustration. The joy of the run was overshadowed by having to send Ziry away. Not only that, it was obvious the other wolf would no longer be able to run with the pack. It was like her five years living in Chicago when she refused to join the local pack or run with them. All those years she'd avoided the other pack because she'd known it would cause issues.

Approaching her pack, she tried to hide her thoughts and feelings from a group brought up to sense emotions in others. She sighed and thought about all the discussions that would be happening the next day.

Chapter 16 - The Birds and The Bees
Ziry

The obnoxious beep of Ziry's alarm woke her up while it was still dark outside. She wanted to go back to sleep. It wasn't as bad as if it were five in the morning back home, but it was still early ... dark as pitch outside. On her run home last night, guilt filling her wolf body, a form ill prepared for such an emotion, she'd tried to figure out what had happened with Joyce and Orin, but it wasn't anything she'd ever heard about. She'd run with her family's pack for years and had never had wolves try to link with her as alpha before. The guilt still nagged at her, but more philosophically. She'd have to call her parents later today ... unless Tamsin was about to have words with her.

With a groan, she dragged herself up, did her morning bathroom routine, then slipped on jeans and a T-shirt. She didn't need anything fancy for the day.

In the kitchen, not only did she find coffee already brewed, she found Tamsin, a wary look on the alpha's face. Ziry set her jaw, ready to face the proverbial firing squad. She'd fucked up the night before and it was time to figure out how and why.

"Morning, Ziry. I think we should talk." Tamsin took her mug of coffee and sat at the kitchen table. With a sigh she sipped her liquid ambrosia.

Though Ziry knew this was coming, she'd hoped to put it off for a few days. Her mind spun and she didn't know what to say.

With a sigh, she found a large mug, filled it with the dark delicious coffee she was learning this pack was famous for making, added a splash of milk, then sat down at the table across from Tamsin. "Sure, we can talk. I'm guessing you need to get to work and don't have a lot of time."

"My first class starts at nine, so I'm good." She sipped from her own mug. "Have you run with many other packs?"

Ziry shook her head. "No, mostly with just my own in South Dakota. When I was younger, I traveled around to meet all the packs, but that was a long time ago."

Tamsin sighed. "That's what I thought. You're a powerful alpha. Your wolf recognizes your parents for who and what they are, but when you're anywhere else, she wants to show dominance. We have a few choices. We can fight, which I really don't want to do. Or, if you're here for another full moon, you can head down the coast and run alone."

Ziry sipped her coffee. She knew the right answer, but she was so tired, forming the words took more effort than she felt she could muster.

"Do you know why it was those two wolves that were drawn to me?"

A small chuckle. "Funny you should ask. Next time you talk with your parents, ask about Joyce and Orin. They used to be part of your pack. When the black witches attacked, they didn't kill the kids. Joyce ended up in Wisconsin with a scholarship to college, Orin ended up here."

Shock reverberated through Ziry. "Really? They were originally from South Dakota?"

"That's right. It's taken some time figuring it all out, but they were two of the original survivors of that attack."

Ziry tilted her head, thinking. "I'll have to talk to them about what they remember. So much of our history was destroyed."

"You should. I think Joyce is your best bet." Tamsin gave her a small smile. "Now, if you're here in a month."

"I'll run where you direct me to run, got it. I never knew that was an issue." *One more thing to learn before leading my pack. They should make a manual and stop assuming we all just know everything!*

One of Tamsin's eyebrows rose. "You should know that. It's one of the reasons when lone wolves won't join a pack they're given such restricted areas to live and run. You never know when one of them is an alpha."

"Huh, that makes sense."

The two finished their coffee, and then Tamsin grabbed a bag off the counter before heading out. Ziry contemplated breakfast when Maria came in, poured herself some coffee, then joined her at the table.

Ziry gave the other woman a small smile. "Morning. I was hoping to talk to you about breaking into the black witch lab."

Maria's eyes widened. "Did you find it?"

"I think so. There were a few options, and I've been looking them over."

"Hold on." Maria's hands flew up. "I see why you'd need me, there could be electronic traps, but we should bring Easton in as well. He's always been in security."

Ziry nodded. "Sounds good to me."

Maria headed out, returning with a taller man who looked like he was an old time surfer. Blond hair, blue eyes, and an easy smile. He winked at her. "I hear we're breaking into a place."

Chapter 17 - Walk on The Wild Side
Rho

The day was warm. Rho and Sage decided to hike in the arboretum near the university. As they walked, Rho pointed out her favorite plants. The shade of the trees provided a nice relief from the high sun. For a Saturday in January, the day was oddly warm.

Sage fanned herself. "It wouldn't be so bad if there was a breeze!"

Rho smiled. "Oh, I can do something about that!" She moved her hands a bit and a small breeze ruffled their hair. She tried not to move too much air—it would zap all her energy—but she could do a bit.

"Oh! That's fantastic! I forgot you were an air witch." Sage sighed, lifting her arms to maximize her exposure to the refreshing breeze.

"I try not to push my limits, but today is a necessity."

"I agree." Sage's voice almost came out as a moan.

They continued down the path. Another couple passed them in the other direction, but besides that, they were alone in the serene outdoors. Rho enjoyed looking at the different plants.

Sage lightly traced her fingers down Rho's arm. "How have things been with you this week? Any issues at work? With the coven? Don't forget, you really can talk with me ... tell me anything. We're friends."

Rho dipped her head and hunched her shoulders. "Oh, you know. It was a week. I did a bit of window shopping."

"Do you like to shop?"

"I do. Tamsin and Paige, you know, the wolves, they're getting married in a couple of months. Anyway, they asked if I could help with the wedding dresses."

Sage's mouth dropped open. "I don't know if I should congratulate you on such a great gig or feel bad for the clients you have to work with. I hate working with the wolves."

"Oh, I don't know. They seem nice."

Sage shivered. "But they're wolves. You should charge double for having to work with the dogs."

"I don't know, that seems kind of rude." Rho couldn't believe what Sage suggested.

"Have you quoted them a price?" Sage waggled her eyebrows. "I mean, what they don't know ..."

Rho had to work to keep a blank face. "I have. It was part of the initial discussion. Oh, well." She tried to sound disappointed. "I guess I'm out of luck."

"Yeah, that sucks. Better luck next time. Either double pay, or just say 'no' to them." Sage shivered again, then made a gagging motion. "I avoid working with them like the plague."

Rho knew she would blow her cover if they continued talking about the werewolves. She'd respected them her whole life. She bristled at Sage speaking poorly of them. "Do you want to see any other magic?"

Sage shrugged. "Sure. I mean, we do magic all the time. Unless ... do you want to see some of *mine*?"

A shiver of fear ran down Rho's back. What magic would a black witch show her? What damage would it do? "Okay, yeah. That sounds great. I can't remember you doing any magic during the coven meetings."

A sly smile crossed Sage's face. "I usually hold back, letting others show off. It allows me to better learn ... you know. We're the younger witches, education is the name of the game."

Whereas that was true, part of the learning process was doing. Rho just widened her smile. "Of course!"

Sage performed some hand motions she'd never seen before. A flower, small and stunted, began to get bigger. It continued until it was full, summer big. Whereas an earth witch could encourage a plant to mature within its natural growing time frame, this was something more.

Rho's fingers were cold with apprehension. "How ... how did you do that?"

"I can't tell you, not yet. But I have a feeling, soon." Wrenching her gaze from the beautiful flower, Sage smiled at her. "Come on, let's keep moving." The other witch had a bounce to her step.

As she moved off, Rho noticed a tree behind her with a couple of dead branches. She didn't think they'd been dead before. She bit the inside of her cheeks to keep the outrage and disgust from showing on her face.

Chapter 18 - Two Saturdays ... It's a Pattern
Ziry

Ziry sat in the living room with Maria and Blake. They were waiting on Easton to discuss the following Saturday and the break in.

Maria sighed. "So, this guy, he's part of this company's IT team, top-notch ... I guess. He was given over to me and this other person I work with for training. They asked us to help with their system security."

A smile spread on Blake's face as she sat back and placed a hand on Maria's thigh. "Butch? This is Butch, right?"

Maria groaned and rolled her eyes. "I told you, his name is not to be mentioned, but yes. Anyway, his company is picking up customers of their own. I was overseeing his interaction with one. The customer emailed him and asked that his email get updated because it was incorrect in the system. So, what did this imbecile do? He *emailed him back to confirm the email.* That's right, he emailed someone to get their email. This. This is what I'm working with."

Blake toppled over on the couch from giggling so hard.

Ziry laughed, then said in a droll tone. "I think I've worked with people like that back home."

Her comment only made Blake laugh harder.

Easton walked in with his husband Dylan. "What did I miss? Laughing about my outfit?"

He wore jeans and a black T-shirt that said, *If You Love Someone, Let Them Sleep.*

Blake shook her head and stood. "Coffee? Tea? Treats? You all talk, I'll serve."

Everyone put in their orders as the blond beauty headed off. Dylan followed to help.

From the break-in of Nia's apartment, they'd narrowed the placement of the chemistry lab down to a half dozen. Ziry had gone out investigating. She'd found the one the black witches were using to mix their death juice. Now, they were going to take it down. She was excited to finally be close to the end.

Ziry worked with Maria and Easton for the next couple of hours to fine-tune their plan. They'd each come up with ideas over the week and now they wanted to bring everything together into a concert of sorts. They needed more than the three of them, but not too many people. They'd need Rho to be with Sage, to ensure one fewer witch on the scene. A lot of pieces to juggle.

They were reviewing everything for the third time when her phone rang. She checked the display and saw it was Rho. They decided they'd done enough for the day, so Ziry answered and slipped out into the backyard.

"Hi, how are you?" Ziry was surprised how excited she was to speak with the other woman. She was only in town for a few weeks, and then she wouldn't see the witch again.

"Good. I just spent the day with Sage. She's heading home. I have the evening free and thought we could ... ah ... compare notes from the week."

Ziry snorted. "Is that what the kids are calling it?"

A soft chuckle came over the line. "Well, I *did* think comparing notes could be part of the evening. I also thought I could make steak and bake potatoes, you know, if you like that kind of stuff. Maybe a salad."

Ziry's stomach told her just what she thought of that idea. "You know just how to sweet talk a wolf, don't you? I could bring pie."

It didn't take long for Ziry to get her stuff back up to her room. She stopped at a bakery for apple pie, then drove to the witch's place. The small apartment was cozy and homey. She'd always lived in pack dens, huge and almost overwhelming, but Rho's place felt intimate and inviting.

The smells of garlic and steak filled the air, adding to the ambiance of home. Ziry wanted to sink in and never leave.

Rho placed the pie on a table by the door, then pulled her in for a hug. Ziry combed her fingers through the other woman's hair and shifted the hug to a welcome kiss. Having Rho in her arms felt like being home.

When they separated, she saw the happy blush play across Rho's face.

"Come, sit. You can join me in the kitchen or sit three feet further away in the living room, probably much more comfortable."

Ziry laughed. "I'll sit at the island, that way if you want help, or a taster, I'm here."

Rho pulled a face, smirking and raising an eyebrow. "You think so, do you? Testing the food? Awfully ballsy of you."

Walking up to Rho, Ziry wrapped her hands around her hips. "I just like to make sure to try the things that I'm sure will taste good. If you want to offer an appetizer, I'm sure you could convince me to spend my time on the couch."

Rho pushed her hips against Ziry as she wrapped her arms around her neck. "Why, Ziry, if

I didn't know better, I'd think you were flirting with me." The vixen began rubbing back and forth against her, her scent filling the air, mixing with the aroma of dinner. "But I'm sure you wouldn't want me to burn the steak."

"Hmm. I don't know, at this point you're giving me pause."

With one more caress with her hips, Rho leaned in for a deep kiss. "You are dessert, not the appetizer. Now, let me cook, devil woman."

The banter lifted Ziry's spirits. After the stress of the last few days, and the confusion of the week, running with a different pack, being with Rho balanced something deep within Ziry. She held on tight for another moment, feeling a need for an almost melding of their beings, before finally releasing Rho.

"Okay, fine. I guess waiting for dessert is acceptable. Since I know that dessert will be delectable ... and I don't mean the pie." She gave Rho a toothy grin as the other woman twirled away and headed towards the kitchen.

It didn't take long for the steaks to be done. As they rested, Rho finished the potatoes, placing the topping options out on her small table. Last, she mixed up a couple of margaritas. Ziry loved watching Rho flow around the kitchen as if cooking were a dance and she were the master in her field.

They sat, and Ziry cut into her steak. It was perfectly cooked, medium rare. She groaned. "I can't remember my last dinner so perfectly presented, and I live in the Midwest! This is beautifully done."

The rosy color that tinted Rho's cheeks matched the shade of her top. Ziry wondered if she stripped it away if the color traveled down her body as well as up her face.

As they ate, Ziry told Rho about finding the location of the black witches' chem lab. She shared that she, Maria, and Easton were putting together a sting for the following week to clear it out. They'd spent time watching it and felt Saturday would be their best bet.

"Are there humans who work there?" She bit her lower lip in her concern.

"Yes. From what I could tell, they think it's just a normal science lab, no death concoctions created. That said, when we go in, we can't get caught."

"What is the plan with the black witches?"

"Well, we need to figure out where they're staying. We hope that the information is somewhere in the lab and that it's found prior to destroying the building. We also hope that the destruction of the lab eliminates all research on this spell."

"You know that isn't very likely." Rho sipped her drink, eyes full of concern.

Ziry finished her steak, savoring the buttery softness of the meat as it melted in her mouth, and the garlicky brilliance of the flavor. "We know. We need to find the coven and destroy all knowledge of what they've been doing."

A shiver visibly ran down Rho's body. "I know it's needed but it's such a cold statement to make." She took another sip of the margarita. "When you go after the witches, will the wolves go alone?"

"I hope not. The witches and wolves are such an integrated group around here. I really hope we can take care of this blight together." It surprised Ziry how much she felt that in this city. She didn't know if there was another city in which witches and wolves worked so well together, but here, they were friends.

"So, I could come with?" One of Rho's eyebrows shot up. "After everything I've learned, I'm very frustrated with the lot of them. Not only are they killing people in Santa Cruz, today Sage did a spell, and once she'd finished, a beautiful tree in the arboretum was half dead. What magic is worth killing?" Rho's jaw clenched and her fists were clenched as she started to get worked up. "Magic is beauty and life, not death and killing things around us for selfish reasons."

Ziry got up and knelt between Rho's knees. She took her hands, gazing up at her. "I'm sorry you have to deal with her. If I could, I'd wrap you up in nothing but me and spend a couple of weeks helping you forget all that death."

Rho smirked. "I'll take tonight. Help me forget her."

Chapter 19 - Nice Isn't Nice
Rho

When Rho woke up, the side of the bed where Ziry had slept was empty, but still warm. Stretching, she tried to ignore the disappointment that the other woman had snuck out without saying goodbye. *Maybe she wanted to let me sleep. She was being polite.* Rho sighed. She couldn't convince herself to be happy, even if that was the reason.

She rolled over to her belly and buried her face in her pillow. She had a bunch of things to do; she should get out of bed. Breathing deeply, she could smell Ziry's scent lingering on her pillows. *I wish this scent wasn't so fleeting.* She shook her head, trying to dislodge the silly feeling.

"That's it," she mumbled to herself. "Shower and off to the coven house. I need to talk to Cinthia."

She pushed herself up and was half out of bed when Ziry popped her head out from the bathroom. "Did you say something? Where do you hide your towels?"

An explosion of lightness and joy hit Rho hard. She knew she should fear how happy seeing Ziry still standing in her apartment made her, but at that moment, she didn't care.

It felt like her face would break from the smile stretched across it. "Towels in the hall closet. Coffee?"

Ziry let her eyes linger up and down her body. "Shower then coffee." Her eyes stopped on Rho's bare chest. It suddenly occurred to her that they'd slept naked, and she still wasn't wearing clothes. "Shower for two, then coffee for two." A mischievous smile spread on Ziry's face before she waggled her eyebrows.

Excitement bubbling in her, Rho nodded. "I'll grab the towels and meet you in there."

When Rho stepped into the bathroom, Ziry was already in the shower, facing into the water. She placed the towels on the counter and slipped into the shower behind the goddess of a woman.

Rho placed her hands on Ziry's shoulders and stroked down until she reached the other woman's perfect ass. She gave a squeeze, then rubbed forward. Ziry leaned in, licking Rho's neck. Reaching out, Rho grabbed a second shower head her landlord had installed during a renovation last fall. "Here, let me help you get clean."

The extra wand had a button to pull water into it and allow a person to rinse hard to reach areas. She waved the wand towards their bodies, Ziry in front. She started at the other woman's chest, then moved down. When she got to her feet, she traveled up between her legs, pointing the water stream up when she got past her knees.

Ziry quivered, groaning and leaning back. Ziry reached her hand back, sliding her hand between Rho's legs, returning the pleasure, her other hand angling the shower head to hit her in the right place.

She leaned her body against Rho's.

Rho reached her free hand around, finding Ziry's breast. She licked and kissed the junction of Ziry's neck and shoulder, biting harder as the pleasure rose.

After Ziry cried out, she turned around, taking the shower head. She pushed Rho against the wall and lifted her leg up over her hip. Leaning down, she pulled her in for a devouring kiss. Then Rho felt the pressure of the water on her sex. *Oh gods above, yes!*

The stream pounded on her and she squirmed. Ziry nibbled on her lower lip. "That's it, I want to see you melt for me." Her hot tongue and sharp teeth traveled down towards her ear. Shivers of desire shot through Rho's body as she trembled against the other woman.

She balanced the shower head between their bodies, pointing the pulsating water towards Rho's clit, then used her hand to probe in and out, continuing to lick and nibble Rho's neck and ear.

As the pleasure increased, Rho's breathing got ragged. Ziry leaned down. "I want you to scream so loud, your neighbors are jealous."

As Ziry's teeth scraped her ear, the shower water shifted just enough that Rho's world fractured, and she did as requested, while Ziry held her up.

Rho arrived at the coven house in the midafternoon. She walked up the steps to the beautiful Victorian home. Inside she found not only Cinthia, but Caroline and Mazzy there as well, sitting in the dining room.

Caroline smiled wide. "Please tell me you know how to play spades. I know you're here to discuss everything with Cinthia, but why not double up, right?"

Amusement filled Rho. *How can anyone not enjoy this coven? Everyone in it is such a fun character.* "Spades is a card game, right? Or are you talking about a shovel?"

Mazzy shook her head. "We *need* a shovel to dig through the crap you're dealing with."

Rho narrowed her eyes. "You're both wolves and mated to each other. You're not partnering up, are you? Talk about cheating."

Cinthia brought a tray with coffee and tea options. "Who would you like to partner with?"

Checking out all the faces, Rho shook her head. "This is one of the psychological questions, isn't it? Well, I'll go with Caroline, if I get to pick."

Everyone shrugged and figured out seats. Mazzy dealt. After the bidding, Rho began to fill everyone in on her time with Sage and even what Ziry had told her.

Cinthia tossed a seven of hearts onto the table. "You're spending more time with the wolf detective?"

Rho shrugged. "We're both working on the case. It only makes sense if we work together, collaborate."

The coven leader's eyebrow rose. "That's it? Nothing else is going on?"

Heat rose in Rho's face. She'd find a spell one day to control that. "I don't know. For now it's a bit more, but she's leaving town once this all gets solved, so I'm trying not to get too involved." *It doesn't matter that I want her scent to stay on my pillows, she's the next South Dakota alpha, and I'm a witch. There's no future for us.* A sadness washed through her.

Caroline snorted. "If you learn that lesson, let me know the rules."

Mazzy smirked. "What, you aren't happy with how things worked out?"

"I'm just saying, like this one, you, too, will be leaving one day."

"You do know I work at a lab ... you are a scientist, and now a wolf. Do the math, my lovely witchy wolf."

They all gaped at Mazzy, who shrugged. "What, I go after what I want, even when she's a bit of a cluttered mess."

Cinthia threw her head back and laughed. After a moment, she sighed. "So, next weekend they'll be going after the lab and want you to keep Sage busy. We'll have to make sure Mazzy or Caroline is there, someone who knows the science. Having a witch for traps wouldn't be a bad idea." She turned to Caroline. "Thoughts?"

"I agree. Not that breaking and entering sounds fun, but I think we need someone there who can throw spells."

Chapter 20 - Sprint To The Win
Ziry

The GPS on Ziry's car updated the directions after she turned right at the light. *In two miles turn left, then immediately turn left. It looks like I'm driving into the ocean, but Wynn told me this is where she used to run before she ran with the pack.*

Over the last month, Ziry had searched each of the different buildings that could house the black witch lab. It took a week of sniffing out buildings to find the right one. Then the real work began. It was time to take the black witches down.

She turned left, and left again, and saw the parking lot. It was a cool Wednesday in March and there weren't any other cars around. She parked, turned off the car, and found a bench that overlooked the ocean. She needed to run, but spending a few minutes enjoying the dark, crashing water calmed something deep inside. *I could learn to love the coast ... if my future wasn't the Midwest. If my future wasn't planned out, maybe I could have a future with Rho.* She shook her head. *Am I imagining myself mated to a witch?*

The day was overcast, and the charcoal clouds reflected on the violent waters below. The wind whipped her hair, chilling her skin. She sat and drank in the day.

Her phone rang. After a quick check of the display, she answered it. "Hiya, Dad, what's up?"

"Just checking on you. Your last run with Tamsin didn't go well, and you haven't had many solo runs."

She huffed. "I'm fine, Dad. I'll spend the time thinking about this weekend when we're finally taking out this lab."

There was a moment of silence and then her dad grunted. "Are you ready to lead this team?"

"I am."

He made an interested sound. "They aren't our wolves. You have that well of alpha power, but that doesn't mean you're *their* alpha, that's Tam. Will she be there?"

Ziry lifted her free hand and rubbed her eyes. "Right now, that isn't in the plans. We'll finalize everything tomorrow."

"If she's there, you'll have to fight to maintain the lead position. They'll all naturally turn to her."

She wanted to snarl. "Dad, I've been here almost a month. I know these people, and I know what I'm doing. Stop worrying."

He chuckled. "I know, love. I'm just worried about you. You're going into a black witch lab; it'll be dangerous. I trust you, but this is the first really big fight you've thrown yourself into."

She slumped. "Don't remind me. I'll think about that after we're all safely on the other side of our win."

His laugh echoed down the line. "That's my girl. Okay, you go and kick butt. It's later here, and we're ready for our run. Mom sends her love and is looking forward to seeing you soon. You've missed two full moons. We're hoping you're back in time for April's singing to the moon."

"Me too, Dad. Me too." Her mind drifted to Rho and how attached she'd gotten to the witch in the short time she'd been in Santa Cruz. As much as she missed her family and pack, she knew she'd be leaving a part of her heart behind.

Once she got off the phone, she returned to the car to stash her clothes. Her shift to wolf was quick, and then she was off.

There was a path to the water. The scents assaulted her, but at the same time were fantastic. Fish, seaweed, salt, all of it. There was a long empty stretch, so she ran. Her paws splashed in the salt water, the sandy surf licking her snout.

As she ran, her mind returned to Rho. They'd spent a few nights together over the previous two weeks. They'd attempted to watch a movie every time, but they hadn't managed to see the movie once. Ziry howled out her amusement. She was willing to miss that silly movie a dozen more times.

I'm getting addicted to a witch. A witch who lives in California. She shook her head and snuffled. *The only solution was to enjoy as much of my time with her as I can.*

She thought about the sting the following weekend and Rho's part. *Well, she'll be safe with Sage, well as safe as anyone is with a black witch. The two of them binging on some cooking show ... and this time Rho will actually get to watch the silly show!*

Chapter 21 - War Party
Rho

Entering the pack house was always strange. The pack den was huge. It had to be to house so many pack members. Unlike the witches, most of them lived together.

Everyone was there to discuss the weekend's operation to take down the black witch lab. They needed to decide who was doing what and where each person would be. There were a lot of players, and it was good for everyone to know what was going on.

Rho came with Cinthia, Caroline, and Mazzy. When they arrived, Rho was surprised when Caroline, now both a witch and a wolf, knocked on the door.

Doesn't she have a room here? Isn't she part of the pack?

She shrugged and smiled sheepishly at the group. "It seems like the polite thing to do."

Paige, one of the wolves Rho knew well, opened the door. "Come in, and again, Caroline, you're family. You don't have to knock."

They followed the alpha's mate. She led them to the dining room. There were people sitting all around the large table, which practically groaned under the food. At one end sat Tamsin. Beside her was Ziry. Rho didn't try to figure out who the rest were, she just sat down with her group.

Down the center of the massive table were sandwiches, platters of fruit, small pastries, and plates with cheese, sausage, and crackers. Some of the pack came up and offered Rho a plate and asked her what she wanted to drink.

In a daze, she mumbled, "Tea, please."

Cinthia massaged her back. "Don't worry, dear, it'll be fine. Everyone here is friendly, even if there are a lot of people you don't know."

Across the table, Ziry smiled at her reassuringly. "Okay, everyone is here. There are a few pieces to the puzzle for Saturday's job. The only part we've figured out is Rho. She'll meet up with Sage early in the day and keep her busy. That will be one black witch we can be sure is out of the picture. If we can get extra information from her, even better."

Everyone turned to Rho, and she blushed. She was used to blending into the background, not being the focus of everyone's attention.

One of the wolves, an older man with blond hair and blue eyes, pursed his lips. "Will she be safe alone with the witch?"

Ziry tilted her head, considering the question. "Rho, do you want to answer Easton's question? I have my opinion, but you're better suited."

Rho's heart began to beat faster, and she bit her lip. Just because Ziry threw her out to the wolves, didn't mean she couldn't do it. With a steading breath, she nodded. "I've been developing a friendship with Sage. She's almost to the point of offering me a place with the black witches ... I think." She scrunched up her face in thought. "We've both discussed our dissatisfaction with things the coven has done, especially the friendly relationship with the pack."

That got a laugh from everyone.

Easton still looked concerned. "Okay, but only if you're certain."

From down the table, a latinx woman half-raised her hand. "I thought my position was pretty set in stone as well. I'm the hacker. I go in and figure out any and all technology."

"True, you are definitely on my team." Ziry continued, "So, back to the other pieces to Saturday's puzzle. There are three other groups. The people who follow the witches leaving for lunch. The driver who brings in the truck, that probably will only be one person—"

"I'll do that!" Paige said quickly. "I'm not really good in a fight, something about my submissive nature and never having been trained. But I'm an excellent driver."

Next to her, Tamsin raised her hand and waggled it in a 'sort-of' gesture. Again, the party laughed.

Ziry nodded. "Okay, so we have a driver for the truck. The last group consists of all the people who come with me into the lab to clear it out."

The room erupted into talk as everyone stated what they wanted to do. Rho listened with half an ear. She had her role and wasn't as interested in what everyone else did. Though she worried about Ziry, she knew the wolves were competent. And in the end, if her part went sideways, she figured the less she knew the better.

Chapter 22 - Well Laid Plans
Ziry

There was a coffee shop across the street from the lab the black witches had set up. The dark wood walls had black and white photos of the area, and shelves held antiques that looked like they dated back possibly over a hundred years.

The café seemed to encourage long stays. It had several small seating areas, as if the local students came in to study often. There was another group on the other side, talking loudly about physics.

Ziry sat at a table with Maria and Easton. At the next table sat Tamsin, Mazzy, Caroline, and Cyrus. They all drank coffee and had ordered the shop's famous breakfast: seasonal fruit parfait with a warm muffin. The flavor of the day was huckleberry. With the number of people in the shop, it was lucky they'd gotten the two tables near each other.

Ziry had been wary of bringing a local cop, but Cyrus promised he could separate his day job from today's operation. "If it weren't for you wolves and my new family, I'd be dead because of these assholes. They're terrorizing my city, and this is the best, if not only, way to stop them."

She'd heard both the truth, and conviction in his voice. His partner, Bexlee, wanted to join in the fun as well, but they decided to limit the number of people on the operation.

Ziry narrowed her eyes at the building. "Every day, just before noon, all the witches leave for a few hours. My guess is it has to do with recharging their batteries before starting a second shift."

After sipping her coffee, Caroline nodded. "That tracks. If they're making the concoction in batches, they need to let it rest. They also need to eat enough to refuel themselves."

Maria nibbled on a muffin. "Does that mean the building will be empty?"

"Oh, to be so lucky!" Easton scoffed. He lowered his voice, though the coffee shop was loud, and it was unlikely anyone else could hear them. "They have humans working for them. We don't know how much they know. They may be complicit in killing innocent civilians."

As they sat, finishing late morning coffee, tea, and pastries, the doors across the street opened and a half dozen people left.

Dylan, Blake, and Orin were planning to follow them. If they could find where the individuals lived, or even better, their coven headquarters, it would help with the next part of Ziry's goal. Destroying the lab and anything to do with the poison killing innocent people was the first step. Then they'd take out the creators.

It was already the first full week of March, and she was ready to get this job done and head home. She admired Tamsin and had been invited to the wedding, but getting home would be just lovely. A pang shot through her at the thought of leaving Rho. She'd become attached to the witch over the weeks they'd been working together, but she was sure their feelings were nothing more than a fling.

"Is that all of them?" Mazzy asked.

Ziry nodded slowly as she watched four drive away in two cars and two walk. "Six has been the magic number every day this week." She finished her coffee. "And I've been here since six this morning; those were the only ones who came in."

Cyrus's eyes bored into her. "If you've been on this place all week, why haven't you followed any of them when they leave before today?" His voice was a low snarl, accusatory.

Tamsin put a hand on his arm to calm him down.

"They always travel as if they are being followed. They're a paranoid lot. Trust me on this. I think they waste their magic on stealthy travel. It's how they've stayed undetected this long. I can't explain it but following them hasn't worked. I haven't found their homes, or a single home, if they're holing up together."

Cyrus snarled. "Then why waste people on following them?" A low growl could be heard deep in his gut as he snatched up his coffee and drank it.

Ziry sighed. "I'm one person. I'm good at what I do, but my ego isn't so large that I'm not above having others try where I've failed."

Maria's phone buzzed. She looked at it, then her eyes widened. "Blake said her pair stopped for lunch a few miles away."

Easton shook his phone. "Orin and Dylan each checked in. Dylan sent a pic. The six are eating at a Mexican restaurant. Outdoor seating. The place is crowded." He checked his watch. "It took them just over twenty minutes to get there. If we figure at least an hour to eat and twenty minutes to get back, we have an hour to get in and destroy whatever we can find."

Ziry nodded. "Okay, let's move. There's a receptionist. If we need to split, remember: me, Easton, and Maria are one group; Tamsin, Cyrus, Mazzy, and Caroline, you four are the other. We don't know if the place is bugged or how many humans there are, so the less we talk, the better."

They got up and put their plates in the bucket by the trash. Easton patted his pockets. Maria tilted her head. "What do you have?"

He cut his eyes to Cyrus. "I know you're here out of uniform, but how *far* out of uniform?"

A low growl came from the cop. "Just talk. In for a penny and all that."

Easton huffed out a laugh. "I have chloroform."

Caroline stopped. "Really? You brought that? You know it isn't like what you see in the movies."

Everyone stopped in a group. Easton narrowed his eyes. "I don't want to kill random humans who may or may not know what they're doing."

"We should've brought more witches," Caroline mumbled. She squared her shoulders and spoke with determination. "I can use a sleeping spell. It's not my strongest spell, but I can do it once, maybe twice."

They all watched as Caroline crossed the street. She entered the building that took up most of the other side, stretching along two roads. As they waited, Ziry considered the lab she'd been casing for the last week. The front had a brick facade with a stylized pattern. The side was a basic light brick.

The black witches' lab seemed to blend in as much as they did.

They were in an industrial area, but all the buildings had character. The door was at the corner. Ziry began to get anxious. She didn't like sending others in blind.

Hands fisted, nails biting into her palms, she'd just decided to go after the other woman when Caroline opened the door and waved to them. The group crossed the street and met her outside the door.

Caroline spoke softly. "The receptionist was alone in there, but I heard talking and movement through the open door, so I know there's others in there. The spell took, so he should be out for at least the hour regardless of noise made."

They headed in. Behind the desk, they found a blond man in a gray suit lying on the floor. There was a door that led to a hallway. Almost directly across from them was another door. Squinting, Ziry thought it looked like there was someone in that room.

Ziry indicated the other group, made a circular motion, then pointed down the hall. She watched them head down the hall and turn at the corner.

Once they'd disappeared, she motioned at the pair with her and then to the office. They moved to the door.

Easton pushed slightly. Before it was more than a few inches open, a word that felt like greasy oil slipped past Ziry's ear sending shivers down her spine. Maria grunted and fell to the floor with a whimper.

Ziry and Easton slammed through the door and found a black-haired woman standing by a desk, her eyes wide. "The interloper from South Dakota and one from here." Her upper lip popped up in a sneer. "You dare invade my domain, dogs?"

A fucking black witch? Seven? There were seven?

Ziry moved left as Easton moved right. The witch's hands, palms out, tracked them. She could only watch one of them. Ziry knew she'd used a big spell to take Maria down. Sleeping spells didn't work on wolves, and she could hear the other wolf struggling. It had to be some sort of binding.

How much magic does she have left? Do black witches have the same limits as the others?

She darted in, ready to fight. The witch turned, a light glowing in her hands.

Ziry slid, like she'd learned in little league when she loved to steal second base. She aimed for the woman's feet, knocking into her. The witch tried to side-step, but the slide had been unexpected, and she toppled.

Ziry rolled, avoiding the glowing parts of the evil witch.

From the corner of her eye, she saw Easton dart in with a cloth in his hands. A plastic bag flitted to the ground behind him. He placed the cloth over the woman's mouth and nose. She struggled, but eventually passed out.

Once she dropped, Ziry moved to Maria. The magical bindings still held her strong. Ziry grumbled under her breath, then turned to Easton. "I don't think she's out. She's playing possum. Once you let her go, she'll attack us."

Easton's face hardened. "Well, they're killing our city. There's only one real solution, right?"

"That's how I see it. Check with your alpha if you want."

His eyes unfocused for a few moments, then he nodded and jerked the woman's head to the side. There was an awful cracking sound, and the witch went limp. Maria slumped, released from whatever held her.

She pushed herself up. "For fuck's sake, that was annoying. You brought me to help, not get caught in ... whatever that was."

Ziry pointed to the desk on which sat a computer. "You can help. Be our hacker."

A smile blossomed on the other woman's face. "Oh, I can definitely do that. Finally, something fun."

They watched as she started to type. "This may take a while. You two should continue to search. I have this room. I'll let Paige know to bring the truck and boxes." She opened a drawer. "There aren't any papers here. I'll check the rest, but the computer is pretty much it."

When Ziry and Easton got to the intersection where the other group had turned right, she noticed they could've turned left, but the lab was obviously to the right. The bright light from the door and the smells were enough to give it away. She was about to suggest they check to the left when a flash of light and a crash had them both running to the lab.

Chapter 23 - Illusionary Wall
Tamsin

Tamsin could feel the tension of all the other people with her. It took all her patience to let Ziry lead her wolves and not take over. She'd invited the detective to do a job, and bickering wouldn't get things done any faster.

After they separated into two groups of four, however, she knew she could relax her hold on her power a bit and take command. She let Cyrus take point as they made their way to the intersection of the two halls. There was a single room to the left. Her wolf told her it was empty; they could check it out later. At the end of the hall the lights behind the door were off.

Facing Tamsin, Cyrus signaled his desire to take the hall to the right, towards the lab. After a slight nod from her, he continued leading the group. They passed two doors, but from the scent and labels, they were just restrooms ... and empty.

The door to the lab was open. Tamsin could hear people moving around. Standing against the wall, Cyrus peered in. He faced the group and held up three fingers. With two fingers, he waved to the left, then with one, he pointed to the right.

Tamsin shut her eyes, imagining the room. She connected to Cyrus to get his impressions of the area.

"You take Caroline and Mazzy, go left. I'll take the single person. Hopefully, this is it for humans."

Cyrus nodded, then signaled the plan to the other two. They slunk into the room. When

Tamsin got to the door, she turned right. The single woman wasn't wearing the same lab coat as the other two ... a leader?

When she got within a couple of feet, the woman turned to say something to the other two, and her eyes widened. Her hands flipped up, knocking Tamsin back, just as the scent of old leather hit her ... *a fucking black witch.*

In the back of her mind, Tamsin felt Maria's frustration. She couldn't deal with it while facing at least one witch. "Is it one witch or more?" she asked the room.

Mazzy grunted, and glass crashed. "These two are human."

The tall woman with dirty-blond hair glared down at Tamsin, then her focus shifted to the others. "Stop them."

"Of course," two voices said in unison. A shiver went down her back at how weird they acted.

Tamsin got to her feet, squatting slightly, ready to charge in.

The woman chuckled. "Oh, dog, do you really think you have a chance? There are three of us, and that's just this room. You didn't bring enough puppies to stop us."

Cyrus barked out a laugh. "We've restrained one of them already. The other has weapons, but we're close."

The black witch's eyes widened, and she glowed a hazy gray. "Fucking amateurs."

When the witch turned to the others, Tamsin leapt towards her. Just as she connected, Easton reached out to her. *"Boss, we have a situation here."*

Tamsin and the witch fell to the floor, rolling midway down. *"What's up?"* She grabbed the witch's wrist, slamming it to the ground, pinning her other arm under her knee.

"We knocked out a black witch in the office. She isn't dead, but if we let her live, she's made it clear she'll come after us."

"Do you think I need my hands to do spells, dog?" The witch glared up at her. She spat, hitting her arm.

"These witches have been killing the innocent. Even if they don't come after us, they'll find more humans to kill. It's like rogue wolves; they've gotten the taste of humans. We have to stop them." Tamsin glared down into pale blue eyes. "Where's your backup, bitch?"

"You're the bitch, dog!" She bucked up hard, throwing Tamsin.

From across the room, an unknown voice filled the space. "Where am I? Who are you guys? What is going on? Why am I in a lab?"

The black witch, on her feet, bellowed. "You killed Narleen? You animals!" Tamsin barely tracked the witch as she reached for the human and snapped his neck. As he fell, the witch held out her hand, a wide-eyed manic look on her face. A cold tension in the air sent chills down Tamsin's spine as the scent of old leather intensified.

As the man collapsed, he visibly aged. When he hit the floor, he was nothing but a mummified corpse.

Bile rose in Tamsin's mouth. The thought of killing and feasting on the power of an ally, on anyone, was beyond horrible. It took her a moment to get her mind around what she saw. She shook her head to get back in the fight.

The witch held out both her hands, palms out, one towards Cyrus, Mazzy, and Caroline, and one aimed at Tamsin. She started to mumble.

Tamsin scooted in the direction of a table, but she saw Caroline doing ... something.

Both witches said a word.

There was a flash, and the table Tamsin had managed to get behind flew, pushing her into a wall. She saw an image of a wall of water explode, drenching her wolves, as the witch bellowed one more time.

The fight was on.

Chapter 24 - Stay Calm and Carry a Big Witch
Rho

Sage pulled up in her pumpkin-orange Mini Cooper. Rho juggled her purse and a bag with pastries as she got herself into the tiny car. She smiled at the other woman. "Should we get you a coffee? I only brought one."

"I'm good. Once we get to my place, I'll put on a pot. What's in the bag?" Sage tapped the bag with her elbow.

"The bakery had amazing looking profiteroles and Danishes. I couldn't resist. I also grabbed a couple of brownies. I wasn't sure what you liked." Rho waggled her eyebrows at Sage. "If you don't like any of the sugars ... more for me."

Sage laughed. "Oh, no, I like all the sugars. Since we're going to be watching a marathon of *'Is It Cake'* I got some cupcakes. I figured we'd be jonesing for something before we got too far into the show."

Rho rubbed her stomach. "Do we have anything without sugar?"

"Whoa! Who's the amateur now?" Sage turned, driving further from Rho's apartment.

Rho watched the houses fly by. Sage drove confidently, but fast. Rho wished she were with Ziry, breaking into the lab. The others were probably at the coffee shop right now. She had a basic breakdown of the plan. They were planning on doing the break-in at about noon. But her job was to keep Sage busy. She was the one black witch they knew about. If the alarm went out, the fewer combatants, the better.

With a laugh, Rho turned to Sage. "I'm just saying, pizza, tacos, something else would be nice, but if it's a sugar coma we're after, then that's what it'll be."

After another few minutes, they reached Sage's place. She lived in a basement apartment of a large, periwinkle house. Despite the stairs they took down to get into her home, there were several high windows that allowed for natural light.

Rho set up the pastries she brought while Sage put on a pot of coffee. Once they both had full mugs, they sat on the couch and started the kitschy, funny show.

Sage leaned forward, looking at the items on the pedestals. "It has to be number five. That has to be the cake."

"The bakers agree with you, look, they showed at least two people selecting that one." Rho bit into a Danish. She had to admit, this wasn't the worst way to spend the day.

From the television, the host asked, "Is it cake?!" Then cut into an ice chest. He'd already stabbed a beach ball and a pile of towels, bemoaning the items not being cake.

Sage shook her head. "Why would they try to make a shell? That looks so hard."

After sipping her coffee, Rho laughed. "I don't know, the ball would be harder, right? It's like a balloon. Or the towels? I think they all look hard."

The competitors started describing the cake they'd make, and Rho's belly grumbled. "Can you imagine being a judge? That's what I want. Just famous enough to be a judge on some of these shows."

Sage sipped her coffee. "Yes! I want skilled bakers competing to make me happy with their baked goods. Is that too much to ask for?"

They both laughed. Then Sage groaned at the cakes being made. "That's it, I'm breaking out the cupcakes."

"Do they look like other things? Or are we eating boring cupcakes?" Rho teased.

Laughing, Sage walked into the kitchen area. Not that it was a different room, her apartment was mostly one large space. "We can pretend ... but really, they're just chocolate and vanilla cupcakes."

Rho sighed. *It's too bad she's a black witch. She seems fun to hang out with ... except for the flower she pulled energy from.* "You know, I'm good with that."

Halfway back from the kitchen, Sage checked her phone. Her face tightened, then she shook her head. "You know what, I need to grab something from my room. I'll be right back."

"Everything okay? You're not going to disappear on me, are you?"

"What? No, why would you say that?"

Rho slumped. "I have a bit of premonition, and everything about you shifted. I don't know, you changed."

Swallowing hard, I shiver. It wasn't just that everything had changed, I need to be on my guard. That premonition changed everything.

Sage's eyes narrowed. "I just ... remember when I told you I could help you grow as a witch, become more than you are now?"

"Yeah." Rho put her mug down.

"Well, it's time to decide. I think ... well, I was told something happened, and I may be heading out of town for a day or two. I'd like you to come with me. You could learn about my group. They'll help you grow as a witch, become more, become stronger, but you'd have to ... Rho, you'll have to trust me. Do you trust me?"

Fuck no! A shiver went down her back. She couldn't let Sage out of her sight. This was her job for the day. "Of course I trust you, we're friends. You've been so nice to me these last few weeks, I don't know what I'd do without you." The words felt foul in her mouth, professing faith in a black witch. She didn't like lying, but she knew it was the only way.

After staring at Rho for what felt like an hour, Sage nodded and dug her phone out of her pocket. She pulled her gaze from Rho and navigated for a few moments, then put the phone to her ear. "Hi, what happened?" There was a pause. "No, I'm not alone, but I think Rho's ready." A longer pause as she listened to whomever was on the other end of the line. Finally, Sage nodded and put her phone in her pocket.

She started cleaning up. "Something happened. I don't have all the details, but I need to meet up with my ... *other* sisters. I'm going to need to bring you with me ... it's, well, it's the safest option."

A spike of fear stabbed through Rho. "Are you asking me or telling me?"

"Well, technically I'm asking you. I don't think I could force you. I just think it's the right choice." Sage gave her a sheepish smile.

There was so much criteria to consider, but she didn't have time to weigh it out. Sage's piercing gaze bored into her, demanding an answer. Taking a shaky breath, Rho nodded. *We need to find their hideout. This may be the only way. I can call, or they can track my cell phone once I'm there. This will be perfect.*

A smile spread on Sage's face as she took Rho's hand and led her back out to her car.

Chapter 25 - Black As Night
Ziry

Water spilled through the door as they reached the threshold. Ziry ignored the puddles of liquid as she saw the wolves tight, in fighting form, and a stranger secured to a chair. To the left, a woman standing in front of her, and ... *where is Tamsin?*

She ran towards the woman, releasing all her alpha power. The woman's pale blue eyes widened. "Another dog, excellent. I took care of the other one. Was she your second?"

Behind her Easton gasped.

Ziry snarled. "Ignore her, help the others."

The woman held up her hands, palms towards Ziry, spinning them slowly outwards in tight circles. The air between them seemed to thicken. Ziry stopped. She tried to step backwards, but it felt like she hit a solid wall. Only the path ahead was open.

The witch's eyes glowed dark gray. "It's just you and me, puppy, and when I'm done with you, I'll have dissected you, learning your secrets. I'll be the one to figure out the secret of werewolf healing." She sneered. "Fuck killing humans. The power filling the air is great. My coven is more powerful than any other with our controlled deaths, but I'm the smartest leader of any coven. I know more science. And you're going to be my poppet."

Ziry snorted. "Are you monologuing?"

The other woman's hands stopped moving. She pulled one back like a whip, bringing her fingers together. Ziry was yanked forward, falling to her hands and knees.

Behind her, Ziry heard scuffling, but it was low and muffled, as if coming from under water. She hoped the people behind her were doing okay. It seemed like this witch was the last person standing, but there could be others.

The witch sashayed over to her, smirking down like a benevolent overseer. "You'll be my test subject for a very long time, dog. Are you as excited as me?"

Ziry spun, kicking out her foot and sweeping the witch's legs from under her. She squawked and windmilled her arms as she toppled down.

Completing her rotation, Ziry launched herself onto the other woman, pinning her arms. After a moment's hesitation, she reached down, and took her enemy's head in her hands. Arms shaking, Ziry started to squeeze, but bile filled her mouth at the thought of killing a person. She'd never done it. She knew it had to happen, but this would be her first kill. *Damn it, I'm an alpha! I protect the people around me.*

Dark eyes narrowed at her. "You can't do it, puppy. You're playing the leader, but you're too soft. If you were a witch and came to me for training, I'd just kill you and use your death for more power. Not that someone as weak as you would give much."

Ziry snarled. "I'm not weak. Being compassionate isn't a weakness, bitch."

The other woman laughed and tried to buck her off. Having older brothers, Ziry scoffed at the attempt. "Is that the best you have?"

"How long are you keeping me here before I can start my tests, puppy?"

Tightening her jaw, Ziry realized there was only one way this could end. All her training had led to this, and if she wanted to be a leader, a protector, someone others could look to, she had to make the next move. After taking a steadying breath, she squeezed her hands tighter, feeling the silky hair under her fingers, and the ends of the left ear. Trying not to think about the person behind the evil, she twisted as hard as she could.

As the crack reverberated through her, sounds came to her from the rest of the lab. Someone grunted, as if they'd fallen on the floor, and a piercing scream stopped abruptly, replaced by confused mumbling, and scared questions. It sounded like Cyrus was helping whomever it was.

"Are you okay?" Tamsin's voice reached her. *She's okay! Of course the piece of shit black witch lied.*

A warm hand landed on her back. "Ziry, are you okay?"

"Yeah, I ... it's my first kill. But yes. It needed to be done." Ziry's body trembled, and she swallowed back the bile, still filling her mouth. She knew Tamsin heard the lie, but thankfully the alpha let it slide. She *would* be okay, she had to be. This was one of the responsibilities of leadership: protection.

Tamsin massaged her back. "You did well. Usually it takes more than one-on-one combat to take down a black witch. You caught her by surprise and acted on her prone position as well as her huge ego. That was well done on your part. For what it's worth, I'm proud of you."

"Thanks." Her voice came out shaky. She realized her hands were shaking as well.

From behind them, a knocking came on the wall. Paige popped her head through the door. "I have the truck ready to fill."

Caroline laughed. "Oh, we have plenty of things to fill it with."

Rho gazed at the death around her and thought about the amount of work it would take to empty the lab. *Well, at least Rho is safe watching that silly baking show.*

Chapter 26 - Dash Away Little Rabbit
Rho

They drove up Highway 9. "Where are we going?" Rho asked. She'd asked before, but Sage had waved her off saying 'later.'

"East. We're almost there." Sage was focused on their route, barely paying attention to Rho.

Sage pulled off and headed down a small road. That road led to another and yet another. As they went, Rho's heart beat faster. *Will I have reception?*

Will the others be able to find me? It took an effort not to wring her hands.

Eventually, Sage turned and went up a long winding driveway that ended at a low-slung white house. She parked and unhooked her belt.

Rho let out a burst of breath. "Good, we're here."

"Not quite. We'll have to walk for about two miles. There's a more direct way to get to my coven's meeting house, but it's secret. Until you've sworn in, we need to take the long way. There's a small bunker that we'll stop in. I can answer a lot of your questions, and you'll meet more of the others."

"A ... did you say, 'bunker?'" For some reason that didn't sound good ... or safe. Easton's question came back to her, and she started to wonder if she'd been cocky in her answer.

Sage reached over and rubbed her arm. "Don't worry. It's just a place out of the elements where we can talk. I have so much to talk to you about and show you." She turned to Rho with an almost maniacal smile. "Do you trust me?"

Do I trust you? For fuck's sake, no! How can I trust someone who uses death as a power source?

Someone in a group killing innocent people? What a stupid question. She unhooked her belt and shrugged. "Sure, yeah. I'm here, aren't I?"

They got out and started walking. The woods were still with the sounds of birds and rustling animals. Rho couldn't see a discernible trail as Sage walked forward with determination.

There were some twists and turns in the path, not all around trees, and again, Rho wasn't sure how Sage knew the route. She feared asking and just followed.

Eventually they got to something that looked like a storm basement door set in the ground, without a house anywhere near. There was a lock on the door with a code. Sage blocked Rho's view as she unlocked the entrance and opened up a hole with a set of stairs.

"You can make a light ball, right?" Sage asked.

"I can."

"It's one way we can test that only witches come down this way."

Rho followed, biting her tongue. *Do the black witches understand how flashlights work?*

Once they were beyond the doors, Sage closed them. Rho heard them click with a secure sound.

"Are we locked in?" She debated summoning a small ball of light but wanted to preserve her magic.

"Oh, yeah. We take security seriously, but don't worry. It isn't like you're a prisoner." She chuckled. "You can leave at any time. Come on. There's a room down here with couches and a fridge. We can get something to drink and talk."

There were thirty-two steps. The hallway wasn't very tall or wide. Rho could reach out and touch both walls. They went through a door which had another key pad. Once through, Sage turned on the lights. They were in a large room with two areas. One had three couches, two recliners, and a television. The other was a small kitchen. There were three doors.

Sage went into the open center and spun. "Isn't this place great? Let's get comfy and we can talk. Are you hungry?"

As much as Rho regretted coming and her stomach churned with nerves, she knew she had to keep her strength up, show Sage she was on her side. "Oh, food would be good. The desserts we ate earlier were not enough."

"Right? Okay, I'll stick a pizza in the oven." She went to the freezer, pulled out a pizza box, looked it over, and then turned on the small oven. She then faced Rho, her face bright and open. It felt fake and made Rho nervous. "Don't just stand there, come, look around, find something to drink. Make yourself at home."

Nodding slowly, Rho walked into the kitchen and opened the fridge. It was stocked. She reached in and took a can of soda. Sitting at the table, she tried to relax. "How long will we be here?"

Sage shrugged one shoulder. "That depends. While the oven warms up, let's talk." Her eyes widened and her shoulders tightened as if what she was about to say was very important to her. "Here's the thing, I'm part of another group of witches. I think you've figured that out. But my group is different from Cinthia's, stronger." She gazed off for a moment. "Better."

"Isn't all magic the same?" Rho asked, brows knitting. She didn't want Sage to know she knew.

"You would think, but what you've been taught is too restrictive. There is a whole world of magic that the covens have hidden from you," she quivered as her eyes grew brighter. "Did you know that you can set a bigger spell, like freezing the air into a box to hold enemies away from you? Then you can close the spell off with a trickle of power. Holding the spell engaged without actively having to think about it. Only my branch of magic can do that." Her face broke out in a huge smile, drawing Rho in with her excitement.

Rho's mouth dropped open. This was new. "You can set a spell and hold it in an infinite loop without draining all your mojo?"

Sage threw her head back and laughed, then the oven bell dinged. She continued to giggle as she put the pizza in to bake. "Exactly. A spell can be put in place, and the only things that will stop it are either the will of the witch or, of course, the witch's death."

"But, Sage, what is this kind of magic? When I was a kid I heard about this. My mother told me that she knew of a woman whose mind had been taken over by a witch, and this sounds very similar. But that was done by a black witch." A chill made Rho shiver. She wanted to push the topic, but the memory still made her nauseous.

The woman had been her aunt and when her aunt's mind had been returned to her, she had no memory of the six months it had been taken over. During that time, Rho's mother and her family had all but disowned her aunt. She'd changed, become distant and mean. Unrecognizable.

A spatial witch, who could reach in and read her memories back through time, who found the touch of the black witch. They learned that her aunt worked at a bank, and they wanted to use her connections to embezzle money. It took power, hacking, and more money to fix what the witch had done.

The family never found the witch who attacked her aunt.

Sage nodded. "Taking over someone's mind is pretty easy. It doesn't take a lot of magic. When you get skilled as a black witch, you can usually control two humans with ease."

"Two?"

"Yeah. It's odd that someone went after a witch. That isn't normal. I wouldn't try. I don't know that I could capture another witch's mind, not alone, much less hold it." Sage sounded awed.

"It sounds like controlling human minds is common."

"Well, yes and no. We have a lab with four human workers. We've been working in rotation, keeping two witches on site at all times. The two living there have stayed there for the last two months. They'll probably be switched out in another week or two. Switching the ones controlling the minds is a process."

"A lab? Like a science lab?"

Sage slowly nodded.

"So the workers, they're professionals? Scientists?"

"I guess." Sage bunched up her shoulders in a small shrug.

Heart beating faster, Rho tried to sort through her questions. "They have to live there? Can they ever leave?" she was gob-smacked at what Sage thought was normal ... okay.

"They can leave, but not for more than an hour or two. The workers, um, scientists, have strong minds, and we need them to stay focused on the work."

Rho lifted her hands and shook them. "Wait, we're getting off topic." She decided she couldn't focus on the humanitarian aspect. If she did, she'd break her cover. What Sage said disgusted her too much to keep up a façade. "Black magic. Don't you use death for your power source? I mean, isn't that just wrong?"

"You do know that death can be from plants that are on the tail end of their life or from animals that just died. It isn't always about killing." Sage shook her head, seeming disappointed.

"But sometimes it *is* about killing, right?" Rho knew she shouldn't push, but her mind reeled, and this was just too important to drop.

"Sometimes, but most of us are good people who just want more powerful magic."

"So, you're telling me you don't kill people?"

Sage's face softened with a gentle smile. "Of course not."

I have never wanted the wolf's ability to hear or smell a lie so much. "So, what's that lab for? Why control the scientists?"

Sage's smile grew. "That? We're mixing magic with science so that humans can benefit from what we have. We're trying to help heal the world. We can't just let the humans walk away with the knowledge there's magic, now can we?"

"So, you're out there bettering the world?" Rho tightened her jaw, forcing herself to stop before she added any opinions to her question. She hoped Sage didn't hear the flatness of her question.

Apparently lost in the excitement of recruiting another black witch, Sage whole body exuded happiness. "Of course we are. What else would we be doing?"

Cold dread washed through Rho's body. She couldn't imagine *what* the black witches' thought would make the world a better place. Whatever it was started with a lot of death. Her mind flashed to Ziry and the lab. *At least the others will find the information we need. Hopefully all of this will come to an end soon. I wonder if the lab was empty.*

Chapter 27 - Grab And Go
Tamsin

Tamsin's body felt a bit battered from being slammed between a wall and a table. That said, she felt better than she would have if she'd taken the magical blow without a barrier.

She stood, leaning against the wall, breathing hard.

Ziry darted in. She ran towards the black witch and released a blanket of power ... so much power. The witch's eyes widened. "Another dog, excellent. I took care of the other one. Was she your second?"

Tamsin scoffed to herself. *I'm no one's second, bitch. I'll show you who has power!*

Before she could move, she heard a gasp, and turned to see Easton run into the room, eyes on Ziry and the witch.

Ziry snarled. "Ignore her, help the others."

As Easton turned towards Caroline, Mazzy, and Cyrus, the witch lifted her hands, palms towards Ziry, and spun them slowly outwards in tight circles.

That's enough. Tamsin pushed the table, and it fell with a resounding crash. Everyone but Ziry and the witch turned towards her. She felt the elation from her wolves as they realized the witch had lied and she was fine.

With a grumble, she rolled her eyes at them, and waved at Ziry and the witch. "Black witch, they lie."

The others started trying to question the human who was tied to the chair. They didn't see a fourth human come from around the corner, carrying an iron rod of some sort. "Cyrus, behind you."

As the group turned, Tamsin went back to worrying about Ziry. She realized she couldn't hear anything, and the young alpha-to-be was on her hands and knees. Tamsin ran over and hit what felt like a solid wall. The witch had done something to the air.

Suddenly, Ziry spun, and the witch was on her back, but the air was still thick as cement. Apparently, once the spell started it wasn't about to end without some decision on the witch's part.

Tamsin pounded the invisible barrier and snarled. A crash from behind her got her attention. She turned to see what had happened.

The iron rod was rolling from a table. Scientific equipment littered the floor. In front of the table stood Easton in wolf form, his pale gold wolf snarling at the scientist. Caroline and Mazzy held the woman who started to scream bloody murder. She didn't say any discernible words, just shook her head, her lank brown hair slapping the two women as her voice rang out.

Tamsin reached out to Easton. *"Why the form shift?"*

"She has a gun under her lab coat. I wanted to scare her enough that she wouldn't reach for it."

Within the incoherent screams, Tamsin made out the words "man" and "wolf."

The man they'd captured before scrunched up his face as if he wanted nothing more than to cover his ears. *I'm with you, bud, totally with you. If I didn't need my hands right now...*

Deciding everything seemed to be handled, Tamsin turned back to Ziry and the wolf. Despite the thickened air, she could smell Ziry's fear and determination. The woman was fighting an internal battle as well as an external one.

Tamsin beat on the air. She needed to get in and help. *Has she ever been in a fight like this? Does she realize it's a fight to the death?*

A tremor traveled down Ziry's body, and then she grabbed the witch's head and twisted hard. The crack couldn't be heard through the thickened air, but as soon as the bitch was dead, Tamsin fell to her hands and knees as the invisible barrier disappeared.

The stunned terror Ziry felt wafted up to Tamsin. She ran over, asked the other woman how she was. When she didn't answer, she softly rubbed her back, giving her a sense of pack, even if it wasn't her own. "Ziry, are you okay?"

After a moment, Ziry shook her head and took a shaky breath. "Yeah, I ... it's my first kill. But yes. It needed to be done."

Sadness filled Tamsin. Such a hard 'first' to have, especially away from your own pack. "You did well. Usually it takes more than one-on-one combat to take down a black witch. You caught her by surprise and acted on her prone position as well as her huge ego. That was well done on your part. For what it's worth, I'm proud of you."

"Thanks." Her voice came out shaky.

From behind them, a knocking came on the wall. Turning, Tamsin saw Paige pop her head through the door. "I have the truck ready to fill."

Caroline laughed. "Oh, we have plenty of things to fill it with."

Tamsin got up. "Caroline, Mazzy, you two take this room."

"Where am I? Who are you? Why is there a dog in a lab ... and ... um ... what day is it?" The woman stared around the lab, confused. Then she screamed ... again. "Is he dead?"

Caroline sighed. "I've got the humans, if Cyrus can help me. I can clear their immediate memories, and he can get them to somewhere safe. Then I'll help Mazzy."

Tamsin nodded.

Ziry cleared her throat. *Oh, yeah, this is her operation.* Tamsin gave her a sheepish grin before taking a step back. Ziry gave a slight nod of understanding. "Sounds good. Tamsin, if you can withdraw to the outer area of the building, there are storage rooms, I believe, if you and Paige can search and destroy, that would be great. Then the rest of us can do the heavy lifting. I'm going to go check in with Maria and have her gather whatever electronics she thinks are important."

Tamsin nodded. "I assume destroying the place is on your docket?"

"Oh, yes," Ziry agreed. "Each room will be stripped and destroyed. We don't have much time. I don't want to have to fight six more witches, though I think we got one of their leaders."

Outside the lab, Tamsin and Paige found the first room. It was full of the concoction ... hundreds, thousands possibly, of vials of the deadly substance. She wasn't sure how many. There were boxes and boxes full of the stuff. The black witches had obviously planned on relocating this operation beyond Santa Cruz.

Tamsin and Paige started moving the boxes to the truck. They'd destroy them later when they had time and a more secure location. Paige's face scrunched up. "Do you think they were planning on sharing with other black witch covens?"

She snorted. "Sharing doesn't seem like the black witch way, but maybe."

Behind them, Mazzy carried some lab equipment. "It isn't that far off. Black witches aren't wholly awful to each other. It is completely possible that they'd share the concoction but not the process. You know, sell it to make money and extend their control at the same time."

They took everything from the lab, which wasn't much, the storage area, which had a lot of boxes, the office and reception area, which were a few computers. In the cold room, they destroyed everything. They found the latest batch brewing. In a second storage area there were two file cabinets. They took those for good measure. The lightness of them led Tamsin to think there wasn't much inside.

In a last minute decision, they collected the two black witch bodies and left. They weren't sure if the other witches could use their death, or if another witch's death gave extra power to them, but none of them wanted to take the chance.

In the truck, Paige drooped. "So, two dead witches and one dead human. That was better than it could be, but not as good as we'd hoped."

"Exactly. Ziry ran a tight op. Now it's up to Maria to hack the technology. We need to find where these people are living, unless Cinthia's witch has found them. And for Mazzy to mass produce that cure. You know we didn't get all of the death juice. It's still out there."

Chapter 28 - Nothing To See Here
Ziry

By Thursday, Ziry knew something had to be wrong. She and Rho weren't *dating* dating, but they'd kept in better contact than this. Ziry had tried to get ahold of the other woman, but all her calls had gone to voicemail, all her texts had gone unanswered.

Something has gone wrong, I know it. That fucking black witch figured out she was double-crossing her and hurt her. A shiver ran down Ziry's back and her stomach clenched. Within her, her wolf howled in frustration. It had been too long, and the waves of sudden fear were driving her mad. *What if she killed her for a spell?*

Trying to keep herself from spinning out of control, Ziry found Cinthia's number in her contacts and called the witch leader. The other woman answered after a couple of rings.

"Ziry? Can I help you?"

The woman's voice soothed her. "Hi, Cinthia. I know I'm probably overreacting, but I was wondering if you'd heard from Rho. I haven't since the lab take down on Saturday, and the lack of communication seems odd."

There was a moment of silence, and then Cinthia sighed. "You aren't overreacting, dear. No, I haven't heard from her, but I don't think she's hurt, if that helps. I don't know for sure, of course, but if I were to guess, I'd say she was ... pensive."

Ziry dropped onto her bed. "Are you part wolf?"

Cinthia laughed. "No, but I do have an ability to sense things ... an understanding of the universe, so to speak. It isn't perfect. Today, it's telling me my witch is currently okay. That said, don't drop your concern ... find her, please."

Once off the phone, Ziry let herself tremble with the cessation of her belief that Rho hadn't survived. *She's alive. Thank the gods.* Once she could breathe, she headed down to the kitchen to get coffee. Tamsin was there with Orin and Georgette. She sat heavily, letting Cinthia's words sink in.

After she'd had a few sips of her morning brew, she turned to the alpha. "I think the black witches have taken Rho."

Tamsin shook her head. "Why do you say that?"

"She's the only one who hasn't checked in. I've tried to get ahold of her to no avail."

The alpha sipped from her mug. "She's busy, you know. She works for that socialite who always has her running around town. Paige and I have had some trouble scheduling with her."

Ziry opened and shut her mouth, uncertain how much to say to Tamsin. Then she shook her head. "You're right. Rho is a big girl who can handle herself. I'm probably overreacting." A worm of doubt wiggled through her. *Am I too involved in this? Do I need to step back? Give Rho space?*

Tamsin checked her watch. "Gah! I have to get to campus to teach. I'll be back tonight."

Georgette watched her dart off, then turned to Ziry. "There's a big social event tonight that the company wants us all to go to. Fancy outfits, schmoozing with clients. Because they're requesting us to be on the clock from five until midnight, we have the day off. Do you want any help from me?"

Ziry thought for a moment. "I need to go through all the stuff we took from the lab, see if I can find their stronghold. Maybe talk to Maria. Find out if she's hacked into the computers yet."

"Maria is in the backyard relaxing. Go, check in with her. Then I'll meet you in the garage, and we can spend the morning searching."

In the backyard, Maria and Blake sat in side-by-side lawn chairs sunbathing. Ziry dropped into one of the small chairs near them. "Morning, Maria."

Maria cracked open an eye. "Heya, Ziry. What's up?"

"I was wondering how the computer hacking was going."

A low grumble came from the wolf as she sneered up at the clear sky. "They have some excellent security on their machines. I'll get there; it's just taking a while. I've also been very busy with work. I've had to do a lot of set up for this shindig we have tonight. My reward is being required to go, attendance is mandatory."

Blake leaned over and kissed her cheek. "I get to go with you, *and* you have the day off. It isn't all bad."

Ziry's insides tensed as she had to rely on someone else, but her wolf pushed her. She explained to them about Rho. Maria sat up. "Well, fuck. I'm really sorry. I saw how the two of you were getting closer. I'll spend a chunk of today focused on the computers, make them a higher priority. Now that the party is happening, I can spend more time on both the hacking and the follow-up searching through the data. Actually, once I'm in, Georgette can help search. She's excellent at that."

Ziry felt better that they had a plan, though she felt a bit embarrassed she'd been seen. She thought she and Rho had been pretty discreet.

Chapter 29 - Witch-ever Way To Go
Rho

Rho took her phone out of her purse and turned it on. *No Reception.* She shook the damn thing, but it didn't help. *Fuck, fuck, fuck, fuck, fuck! Have they figured out I'm in trouble? Are they coming for me?*

At first, she was convinced Ziry would crash through the door every five minutes, but it had been eight days, and now she wasn't even sure anyone knew she'd been taken. For the first few days, she paced the room. It was a nice room, with a comfortable bed, a wood dresser, bolted to the wall, and an ensuite bathroom. Despite the beauty of the soft blues and greens, the room was a prison. She was locked in each night. Her freedom was an illusion.

That's not fair. You're in an underground facility in the middle of nowhere with no reception.

She narrowed her eyes as she turned off her phone and slipped it back in her purse. She'd seen Sage make a few calls. When she'd asked, Sage just shrugged it off. "I have a great plan, service everywhere."

"Can I use your phone? I need to call Veronica, let her know why I've been MIA."

Sage's face softened. "No. You know how it is. You know too much. Until you've sworn in as a black witch, you're kinda stuck. It'll be fine, though, you want this, I know it'll be great."

"I thought you said I could leave at any time." Fear coursed through Rho. She knew she was in a bad place, but in the back of her mind, she kept telling herself she could always walk away. She'd stayed to gather more information, that was her job. Though she'd gone back and forth, she knew deep down the others would find her. But hearing Sage say she couldn't leave, she finally knew the lie for what was.

Sage sat down next to her. "Look, you don't need to be scared. Everything will be fine. Just breathe ... calm down."

Has that ever worked in the history of anyone ever saying that to anyone?

Rho tried to force a smile but was pretty sure she failed. "It's a simple question, Sage. Can I go home? It's been great learning about things here, but it's been over a week. I miss having my own clothes. The extras here are lovely and all, but vacation's over, right? I need to get back to my own life."

The other woman's mouth firmed into a line. "It isn't that simple. You know all about us. You've heard how the fuckin' wolves killed two of our own, probably killed the humans as well. They're the ones that don't care about life. Then they ransacked our lab, stealing everything we'd set up. Do you know what we were doing in that lab?"

Creating liquid death. Rho's face stayed neutral as she slowly nodded. Hearing about the team's success had been a highlight of her time in the bunker. "You and the others explained it to me. You've been working on something that will bring peace to all that take it."

Jabbing a finger into the air, Sage exclaimed, "Exactly! We're bringing something good to people, and the stupid dogs ruined it. I don't even know if you're safe back in the city."

A tall man with short dark hair and dark eyes poked his head into the room. Barry was one of the black witches Rho had met over the days she'd been living at their compound. "Sage, we're having a meeting. You're needed. Your guest is welcome to join, if you think she's trustworthy."

Sage practically danced in her seat before she shot up. "Come on. Let's join the others."

Rho followed along. She hated these meetings—they made her feel dirty. When their leaders spoke, they made it sound so ... reasonable. She understood why the others followed them. Part of Rho was attracted to the power the black magic offered. She'd spent half her time reminding herself why it was a bad idea to take them up on their offer.

After the meeting, she'd take a shower. She didn't like wearing their clothes any more than she liked attending the meetings, but at the end of the day, if she could bring any information back to the coven, it would all be worth it.

They traveled down a few corridors until they got to a large meeting room. There were a few large couches, recliners, beanbags, and a round table with wooden chairs. Though Rho wanted to sit in the corner at the round table, Sage dragged her to a love seat at the side of the meeting with the others.

Besides the two of them, there were eight others in the room. Barry cleared his throat. "Back to where we left the meeting three days ago. We've lost our leader, as well as Narleen and Loui. Nia is in jail and as good as dead. Of the thirteen we need to do major spells, we're down four. If we can replace one with Rho," he gave her a winning smile, "we're still down three."

A shiver of dread washed down Rho's back. She wanted to please him. A need to make him happy washed through her. She didn't want to take the vows, but she did. The back of her mind screamed it was death powering their spells, but sitting in the meeting, she didn't care. She wondered what the vows would do to change her and if she could denounce them later. Would the voice in the back of her head die, like the creatures they killed for their magic?

Everyone in the room turned to her so she forced a smile and nodded. *I hate being the center of attention!*

Beside Barry, another of the older witches, Kandi, shook her head. She had dark curly hair and knowing gray eyes. "We can't get distracted. The fucking dogs started a war and I, for one, am not about to sit back and let that stand." Rho tried to hide a wince at the word 'dogs'. "We have nine witches. We are more powerful than they are, even with their pet spell-spitters. I say we attack them, let them see how it feels. We can worry about Rho afterwards. A week or two won't matter."

Barry narrowed his eyes. "You don't want the extra firepower for the fight?"

"Look, I think Rho is great. She's pretty," Kandi said this as if it were the only thing Barry were interested in, "and I can smell her power, but we're talking about going against the coven she's been part of for a long time. I have trust issues. I say we wait." Kandi's eye bored into Rho. It wasn't unkind, though it wasn't friendly.

Barry blew out a large breath. "Okay, I see what you're saying. We're going against the dogs, but the two groups are pretty tight. Until we truly know Rho is with us, we sideline her."

Sage sat up. "She's with us, I'm sure. She and I have been friends for like ... forever. What, you all don't trust me?"

"Of course we trust you," Kandi said slowly. "We just need to be extra cautious." She turned back to Rho. "You understand, right?"

Rho knew this answer was important. She wanted to sound excited to be there but understanding. Not relieved for the respite. "I am here for you. To be honest, I haven't been with Cinthia's coven that long, I'm a roamer. I've been searching my whole life to figure out what's been missing in my life. That said, if you think waiting makes sense, then that's what I'll do. No arguments from me."

For the first time, the cantankerous black witch smiled at her. "Perfect. Now, let's plan a dog hunt."

Chapter 30 - Circle Back ... Again
Ziry

"If you don't stop pacing around the pack house, I'm going to kick you out and have you circle the neighborhood," Georgette said from one of the couches in the living room.

"I've tried walking around the neighborhood, but it doesn't help. I snarl at random strangers and scare them."

Georgette put down her book. "Have you gotten any of the reports about the number of heart attacks?"

Ziry sighed and flopped into a chair. "Nothing has gone down. Though we've destroyed their stock at the lab, I fear they'd already sent a bunch out into the streets. Who knows how long it will take for the effects to lessen. I'm just glad Caroline and Mazzy have an antidote."

"Me, too, my friend. Me, too." Georgette untucked her legs. "What's your next move?"

"I'm hoping now that Maria has gotten into the computers, either you or she will find where they're holing up. Then we go there in force."

"Maria unlocked the last computer last night. I'll be spending time today searching. We both took the day off to spend on these beasts." Georgette nodded to the kitchen. "I just need sustenance and more caffeine. Once I get started, I'll get lost in the work. Loading up beforehand is imperative."

I could hug Maria.

After breakfast, Ziry tried to read a book, but she couldn't focus on the words. She kept reading the same paragraphs over and over. Giving up, she put the book down and headed down to the living room to see what was happening there.

Blake sat on the love seat reading, and Easton napped on one of the couches. Biting back any comments, Ziry headed down the hall towards the backyard. *How can they just lounge around when Rho, one of our team, is out there and in danger?*

She circled the large space twice before heading back in through the kitchen door and sitting at the large rectangular table.

She found a deck of cards and began a game of solitaire. After losing the first game, she made a cup of coffee and started a second.

Paige walked in. "Hey, I just got a call from Mazzy. She's at her lab. Wanna come with me to visit?"

Ziry shook her head. "No, I'm good."

Paige smiled wide. "Nope, let me try again." She adjusted her stance. "Hey!" She waved her hand. "You're driving everyone here nuts and those working on the computer are distracted by your fretting. I'm heading to Mazzy's lab with you to get an update on the antidote."

Ziry chuckled. "Wow, look at you going all commanding. It looks good on you."

The other woman pointed towards the garage. "Unless you want to walk, to the car with you!" she pronounced.

"Yes, ma'am." Ziry shook her head in amusement as she followed. Only a submissive could boss someone as dominant as her and get away with it. *It was clever of them to send Paige.*

The drive through town was quick. The new lab was small and built in a building that didn't look like a science lab. Paige parked and placed a hand on Ziry's arm. "We should get some food ... for you, for me, for *them*. We're heading into a den of two wolves. I don't know about you, but I don't want to get eaten alive."

This wolf is too much! She missed being around her own pack's submissive wolves. Their tranquility was magic. "Sounds like a plan, boss. Lead on!"

There was a deli nearby. They bought a loaf of bread and asked the staff to slice it. Then ordered two pounds each of pastrami, salami, corned beef, and ham. To the order, they added muenster cheese, cheddar, swiss, and provolone. They found a box with a variety of condiments. Another one had chips.

Ziry sighed, something about the ordinary also brought a level of calm. Taking care of the wolves around her was good. Paige was brilliant. "This all looks and smells so good. I'm sure it will be gone in an instant!"

Back at the lab, they found Mazzy hard at work. She had a human assistant. The four of them sat and started eating. Mazzy texted Caroline, who had a free stretch of time, so she drove over to join them.

"So, when will you come back and join us in cards again?" Caroline asked Ziry.

"Oh, I don't know. Soon, I guess. It was fun. I forgot how much I liked playing," she admitted.

Caroline lightly backhanded Mazzy's arm. "See, I'm not the only one who enjoys playing. Others have fun."

Mazzy chuckled. "I know, I just like teasing you."

After they ate, Mazzy headed to a stack of papers. "I've been making my way through all the invoices they used to stock their supplies. There were so many, it's ridiculous."

Ziry froze. "Invoices?"

"Yeah, the lab needed supplies ... all labs do. Why?"

"Invoices mean payments. Payments mean bills. Follow the money. Where were the bills sent? Did they go to the lab, or somewhere else?"

The money ... follow the money. Ziry's heart sped up at those words.

Mazzy's eyes widened. "I don't know why I hadn't thought of that myself. I'm so used to reading these, I only considered the materials. The first two I checked were billed to the lab, but let's check them all out."

She handed each person a stack. As Ziry looked through hers, they all were billed to a Narleen at the lab. Every single one. She wanted to howl with frustration. Inside her, her wolf trembled with a need to rend an enemy and fight for what was hers.

For a second, she thought they'd figured it out, but no, back to square one.

Paige squealed and waved an invoice in the air. "I found it ... them. I found them!"

Ziry ran over and looked at the sheet. In her hand was a bill statement. In the corner was an address she didn't recognize.

Bingo! Found you. Hang on, Rho. We're coming for you!

Chapter 31 - Turnabout Is Fair Play
Rho

In her second week as a guest of the black witches, Rho had been given more freedoms. She and Sage had walked outdoors, and Sage had shown her more of the wonders of her flavor of magic. It was fantastical. Black magic at its core couldn't do much more than what Rho and the other members of Cinthia's coven or her old coven did. It was only when the black witches tapped into true death that their spells experienced a power boost.

The two had been walking a trail. They'd heard the rustle of leaves and the screech of an animal. Sage's eyes practically glazed over as she reached for Rho's wrist and dragged her in the direction of the fight.

They found a half-eaten rabbit, bloody and gross. A tremor of disgust ran through Rho, but Sage looked like she'd been given a birthday gift. "Okay, here we go. Notice, I didn't kill anything. I'm not a monster, Rho. This animal is good and dead. This is all part of nature and the natural process." She sounded so happy and pleased with herself.

That was true. Rho couldn't place this atrocity at Sage's feet, unlike all the human deaths from heart attacks that had swamped the city. "I never said you were a monster." Again, Rho fought with herself. Power from a rabbit long dead, was that really so bad?

Sage's face hardened as one of her eyebrows rose. "Not in words, my friend, but I saw how you've been secretly staring when you didn't think I'd notice. I collect from the already dead."

What about the tree in the park a few weeks ago? Rho wasn't ready to really confront her. She feared Sage didn't see plants as truly being alive.

After straightening her shoulders, Sage held up a hand, palm towards the poor dead creature. She took a calming breath, and then the air shimmered and the rabbit seemed to age and mummify in front of Rho's eyes. Once done, Sage shimmied, as if the power had to settle in her bones.

"Okay," Sage murmured. "That wasn't a lot, but it prepares me for tomorrow's melee. If we can find another one of those, maybe two, I'll be full to bursting."

"Is that what you do?" Rho's mind reeled. "Walk the forest looking for recently dead animals?"

One of Sage's shoulders hopped in her signature shrug. "It's one way. It works. Everyone has their own strategy." Sage swung her head around. "Come on, let's continue our stroll. It's such a nice day."

Not seeing any other option, and finding the information interesting, Rho followed. She contemplated the coming attack and the fact that she being left behind. *I wonder if they'll leave me locked up, or if this is my chance to escape.*

In the two weeks she'd been here, no one had come to save her.

Do they even care?

After lunch, there was another meeting. Everyone wanted to finalize the details for the following day. Just like the last war meeting, Rho wasn't involved in most of the discussion. She paid more attention because this time they discussed killing her friends.

"Gabby has been monitoring the wolves for several months. Trust her on this one."

Gabby was one of the younger black witches. When the black witch coven decided that Sage joined Cinthia's coven, a lottery between her, Gabby, a twenty-something brunette with green eyes, and Lexi had been used to decide who went in. Lexi looked like she was still in high school with long, straight, sandy blond hair and flat, light blue eyes. In reality, she was closer to thirty. It was only chance that Sage won.

After getting to know all three women, Rho thought Sage was the only one who could've pulled off the act of being a real witch. The other two always sneered at the mention of any other type of witchcraft and downright snarled at the mention of the 'doggies' as the wolves were called.

Gabby rolled her eyes. "I swear, the dogs smell. I could pick one out of a crowd at fifty paces."

Rho knew this was a lie. Only witches with animal proficiencies could tell a werewolf, and only those with a strong affinity. Animal magic was one of Rho's specialties, and she couldn't pick a wolf out of a group without the person telling her. "Do you have an animal proficiency to be able to smell a wolf?"

A hard stare was turned to her. "Look initiate, just because you don't know the way of black witches, doesn't give you permission to talk to me. Once you're sworn in and have tasted our power, you'll understand how we operate. Any black witch, even the babies, and don't get me wrong, you'll be a baby, can tell a doggie on sight. They're obvious."

Rho had to fight her reaction. *Black witches can sense werewolves like a wolf can sense a witch? Holy hells.*

Barry shook his head as his voice snapped out. "Stay on topic, please. I know we aren't going in until tomorrow, but many of us would rather this meeting end sooner than later."

Gabby huffed out a laugh. "Fair. Okay, the pack of puppies eat together every Sunday morning, usually mid-morning, maybe ten. It's the one time the majority of them are together. We can set a spell on their precious puppy pit and take them out."

Lexi moaned. "And as they fall, we'll get stronger. Why the other witches scorn our power source, I'll never understand. Anything that gives power as the fight continues ... goddess above, they're simple. Idiots!"

"Enough!" Kandi snapped out. "We'll deal with Cinthia and her group later. For now, we focus on putting down the dogs."

Sage hugged Rho's arm, smiling over at her. "This is so exciting. I know you won't be there, but trust me, this will be fantastic!"

It was early afternoon, probably just after two or three. Once her phone had died, Rho stopped having an easy way to tell time. She just wanted an excuse to go to her room and hide. The thought of the wolves dying broke something in her.

Survive, Ziry ... please!

Chapter 32 - On The Trail
Ziry

It took a few hours to get everyone organized on Saturday morning. The witches arrived in a trickle, not having a single home that most of them lived in. Her wolf snarled within her wanting to run. They knew where Rho was ... er, the black witches were. It was time to go!

Curbing her impatience, Ziry sat them all down. "I don't know what we'll find. We have an address. From the information on the computers, it looks like there were originally thirteen members of the black witch coven."

Cinthia nodded. "Huh, they kept that much from the original scriptures." The other witches in the group seemed interested. Cinthia continued. "Is there any way we can get the information from the computers?"

"Absolutely," Maria said. "Do you want digital copies, paper, or access to the computers themselves?"

Ziry snarled, the pain from her nails biting into her palms keeping her from biting off anyone's head ... metaphorically, probably. "Can we discuss all of this, say, tomorrow?"

Cinthia smiled a bit sheepishly. "Sorry, information gathering is always interesting."

"Truth," Mazzy said. "We'll be sending copies over to Colorado as well."

With a sigh, Ziry continued. "Usually I'd agree, but we have someone to save. Back to what I was saying. We'll drive up. I want there to be wolves and witches in each car so that we're prepared for anything. I don't think they know we're coming, but if I were them, I'd be watching the pack house ... anything is possible. We need to go in assuming they're waiting for us."

There was a new tension in the air as they absorbed her words.

She quickly formed groups, with Tamsin and Cinthia's help, and hustled everyone into cars. They drove east up Highway 9, then followed side roads to a winding driveway. A house waited at the end of the driveway, but it was obviously a decoy, empty and unused. The place smelled no different from the woods around it.

Ziry and Tamsin circled it, smelling and sensing. Though the grounds were kept neat, there was no indication of human occupation.

They met back up with the group. Ziry nodded. "Okay, we have fourteen wolves here and ten witches. I don't know how far the real compound is, but from here we'll have to go on foot. I suggest four wolves with the best tracking abilities lead the way, and the rest of us follow."

Tamsin nodded. "We're following the scent of black witches. My nose is good, as is Jett's and

Georgette's. Do you want to stay human or go in as a wolf?"

Ziry considered. She'd caught what she thought was a bit of Rho's scent, but it was stale, two weeks old. She dropped to her hands and knees and shuffled around. It took a few minutes, but she found it again, slight, but there. "If someone is bringing clothes, I'll go as a wolf. I think I found Rho's scent."

Most of the group perked up at that. Paige stepped up. "I'll take the clothes. Lead on, my leaders."

The change was quick. Once her snout was close to the ground, Rho's scent blossomed around her. It was still faint, but Ziry would recognize it, feel it in her bones, anywhere. She wanted to howl her need to find Rho to the moon but muzzled the impulse. They needed to be as quiet as possible.

She trotted off, often scraping her nose through the underbrush to find the smell she desired. Other smells—dead leather, sweet pine, eucalyptus, birds, and other animals—assaulted her, but she focused on the vanilla and cinnamon scent that made her heart pound faster.

A tap to her back flank jerked up her attention. She whipped around to gaze into Tamsin's dark eyes. After a moment, she shook herself and took in their surroundings.

Where are the others? Ziry lifted her head to sniff. She couldn't smell them. Then she realized she'd been running too fast for the humans. She hung her head to let Tamsin know she understood.

Ziry couldn't bring herself to lose ground. She let Tamsin and Georgette run back and forth to collect the others, trying to suppress her whines and whimpers of impatience. When everyone had caught up, Ziry continued, forcing herself to move slower. The older scent ended at a storm door. Her muzzle wrinkled in a snarl, baring her fangs. She wanted to smash it in with her ire.

The four wolves circled out. Time was ticking. It was already after noon! They'd gotten lunch on the way out of the city, trying to move as fast as they could, but juggling twenty-four people was hard. Now the afternoon ticked on. They were advancing too slow.

As she snuffled the ground, Ziry only caught the smells she expected. She moved roughly as her frustration rose. Dirt, grass, tree, squirrel, mouse, grass ... everything was as expected.

A yip to her right had her running. Georgette had found the scent of dead leather. The chase was back on. As they continued, Rho's scent returned, and it wasn't two weeks old.

She's still alive. A new pep infused Ziry's gait.

After more searching, hey finally came to another structure. It looked like most of it was underground, but not all. Time to shift back to a form with thumbs.

Once they were all dressed, the plan had them searching in three groups. One led by Ziry, one by Tamsin, and the last by Georgette.

The storm door they'd passed had a state-of-the art lock on it. This door didn't. Maria searched. She had a device that detected ... electrical stuff, and still, it looked clear. *I need to get one of those ... well, learn what it is, figure out how to use it, and then add it to my collection.* They headed in. The hallway split left and right. Georgette's group went with Tamsin.

There were doors on either side of the hallway, and as they looked into each, they found them empty. When they got to the end of the hall, it took a jog to the right. Ziry heard voices. She pulled out her phone and texted Tamsin. `I hear people ahead.`

It took a moment for the response, but Tamsin replied. `Me too. Two-front attack in thirty seconds?`

Ziry sent a thumbs up emoji, and she got her people in position.

Cinthia and Caroline moved up to the front so they could see what they faced. They raised their hands and started mumbling. Caroline had a way to make the witches in the room feel like time was moving slower, and Cinthia was checking for any plants, reversing their lives back to seeds. No reason to give the black witches any extra power.

On all the teams, water witches prepared ice spears to throw near the black witches, which, after their attack, the fire witches would turn to boiling hot steam.

After that round of attacks, the wolves would join in. Two on each team were in wolf form, the rest were in human form to help with communication.

Ziry surveyed the room. Nine people ... no wait, ten. Rho sat in a love seat with Sage. *Fuck, fuck, fuck.*

"Maria, tell Tamsin we need to change the plan. The spears have to be aimed *at* the black witches, intent to kill. Rho is in there. We can't heat them up."

Maria's face paled, but she nodded and sent the message. Ziry circled her group making sure the new plan was understood.

"What the hell?" a male voice said from the room. "Why are the walls warping? Is someone doing that?"

Ziry heard a round of murmurs, most saying 'no' and agreeing that something was up.

There was a crash. "Barry, are you okay?" a woman asked.

Ziry saw a bunch of people stand, though Rho sank deeper into her couch. *That's my girl.*

As soon as people stood, ice spears flew. Three people fell with screams, and the wolves ran in, Ziry fast on their heels with a scream. A black witch's hand flew up, and Ziry was tossed against a wall with force, slamming into a picture, then sliding down.

The room spun as sounds of fighting reverberated around her. A sense of someone near, and a slight buzz in the air had her twisting and rolling until she could get on her feet.

Surveying the room, she saw Cinthia in combat with a sandy-haired witch. She waved her hands, and Ziry saw her mouth move. The black witch went down, eyes wide in shock. The coven witch looked both sad and satisfied.

Her view got blocked by a woman with black curly hair and narrowed gray eyes. Her hands were up. Ziry felt the air tighten around her. *This trick again.*

"You come to *our* house, dog, and expect to win?"

Ziry smirked. "It seems to me that you've already lost a few of yours."

"We're ten strong, mutt." She spit at Ziry's face. A small movement had the spittle flying over her shoulder.

Behind the woman, the fighting continued. It wasn't pretty. She wasn't sure if everyone would survive, but she only saw three people standing that she didn't know. "I think your number is off, bitch, but maybe the black magic has fucked up your ability to count."

Ziry launched herself as soon as the other woman's eyes darted to the left. They were back, and her hands were up, but it was too late. They were down on the floor and Ziry had her pinned. "From what I remember in my last fight, if I kill you, the magical air box goes away."

"What? It was you?" The woman's shock turned into a hiss of disgust.

"Who killed the black bitch in the lab?" A wide smile on her face, Ziry decided she was having fun.

"We assumed it was the alpha. You're a nobody," the black witch spit out.

"You say such pretty last words." Since it'd worked last time, and there were others to help, Ziry tried not to think too hard as she reached for the struggling woman's head. The witch moved way more, believing in a way the black witch in the lab did not, that Ziry had it in her to end her life. The thing these witches seemed to not know was, wolves were strong and adapted quickly to change. Ziry got her hands around the witch's head and twisted.

As happened last time, the sounds of the room rushed back at her. She was immediately tackled again, flat on her back.

She was ready to fight, so it took a moment to realize the person who had her pinned down was also kissing her.

Chapter 33 - One Is The Loneliest Number
Rho

The meeting wouldn't end. Barry said he didn't want the conversation to go on and on, but gods above, none of them would stop talking. Rho sat next to Sage on a love seat, Gabby and Lexi sat on another love seat, The other six older witches sat spread out on three of the larger couches. There was a Tall bar table with chairs in the corner, but everyone chose the couches.

The room was a lounge for studying and talking. This planning session was meant to be low key, friendly, but being in this room gave the excuse to be never ending. Not even the pale blue walls covered with renaissance paintings did anything but annoy Rho.

What do I care, what else do I have to do? I'm here, lost in the woods, and no one cares. All alone with these awful black witches who will go and kill those I love tomorrow. Rho paused, reevaluating her thoughts. *Love? Do I love Ziry? Am I in love with a wolf? Is that possible?*

She sank lower in the love seat next to Sage. *Will I ever see you again, you stupid wolf?*

"Okay, that works," Gabby said. "Though they use the backyard during their meal, it's empty. They don't lock that stupid doggy door either. We can sneak a couple of us in through there as a two-front attack. They'll never see it coming."

Sage's head tilted. "Have you done it? Snuck in the backyard?"

A slow smile stretched across that snake of a woman's face. "I have. The backyard is a point of weakness, as is their fucking ego. Those wolves think they're top of the top, untouchable. We could put poison in their yard as well and none would be the wiser. If we didn't need them to dissect and learn their fucking secrets, I'd say burn them down."

Barry nodded. "That brings up another issue. We should think about bringing in two to five. We have seven cells, so as many as we can bring in safely."

As scared as Rho was to ask, she had to know. "What about the kids?" *I don't know if I can live with myself if I'm associated with a group that could harm Rainy or Stewart.*

"Kids?" Kandi asked, the older leader looked annoyed at her interruption as if *she* was the reason the meeting was going to go longer. "What kids?"

Sage waved her hand. "There are two brats living in the house."

Rho clenched her jaw. She'd never known two kids less bratty in her life. *In through your nose, out through your mouth ... deep meditative breaths. You have to survive...*

Kandi sighed. "Well, fuck. We'll have to find a home for them. Maybe the witches will take them."

Sage nodded. "I know Cinthia will. Also, a couple of the wolves live away from the pack house. They'll adopt them, I'm sure. It'll be fine." She turned to Rho. "Don't worry so much."

Rho rubbed her eyes. *Right, they're just kids losing their parents. No worries.*

Barry shook his head as if he were changing his mind. A kernel of hope started to take root in Rho's gut. Then he massaged his temple. "What the hell?" he demanded. "Why are the walls warping? Is someone doing that?"

Everyone around her murmured, 'no.'

Rho's head started to spin. She recognized the feeling from a cross-magic exercise they'd done to learn each other's skills. This had the flavor of Caroline's magic. She shifted her eyes back and forth but couldn't see anything amiss.

Barry stood quickly but doing that when a witch played with your mind was a bad idea. If he'd stood slowly, it probably would've been fine. As it was, he crashed into the glass coffee table.

Kandi slipped down next to him. "Barry, are you okay?"

Everyone else, aside from Sage and Rho, rose from their seats. They moved more slowly than Barry, as if searching, trying to figure out what happened. Ice darts flew through the door, striking the people standing. Four fell with the ice sticking out of their chests. Kandi, Barry, and Sage all immediately stuck out their hands to collect the power, the air wavering between the dead black witches and the hands of their colleagues? collecting their life force, while the others not hurt dealt with the incoming wolves.

Where is Ziry? Rho whipped her head around searching.

A red wolf leapt on Barry before he could finish and tore out his neck. Rho wanted to scream. The blood made her shiver. Then she saw Ziry. Time slowed as the auburn beauty dashed into the room, ready to fight. Like a gladiator, her face set on a target. Rho's body tensed to run to her, but before Ziry got two steps in, her body flew, like a ragdoll, into a wall, practically at ceiling height.

"No." Rho gasped, frozen, unable to breathe.

Kandi followed to where Ziry fell and the air shimmered. Sage leaned over. "This will be good. Kandi has so much power. That mutt is a goner."

Sage kept talking, but Rho didn't pay attention. Ziry had to be okay.

A boulder took up residence in Rho's throat as she watched. Her body trembled. She knew she should pay attention to the rest of the group that came to save her, help them, but she was riveted. Ziry. She lay so still, her hair tumbled over her face. No. She had to survive. Rho feared that if she took her eyes off Ziry, then she would die.

Kandi looked away as a loud crash reverberated on the other side of the room. Ziry pounced, taking advantage of the moment. Rho stepped towards them, the crash and screams of the others all around her barely registering. *Please oh please, survive. I have to tell you how I feel. I've waited too long to see you again, wolf.*

A wolf ran past, and a woman fell in her path. Without seeing who it was, Rho stepped over the fallen. She had to get to Ziry.

She hit the wall of air and leaned into it. There was no way through. She pounded, snarling in frustration. *Survive, Ziry! Don't leave me.* She sniffled, holding back tears. Ziry looked like she had the position of power, but she didn't know.

Suddenly, the air released, and Rho ran, tackling Ziry, landing on top of her.

Without caring about anything or anyone, she kissed her—her wolf, her love, her Ziry.

Ziry tensed for a moment, then wrapped her arms around Rho and returned the kiss with interest.

Lost in the feel of finally being with Ziry, the two missed the end of the battle. Behind her, she heard, "Really? This is how you two battle black witches?"

Rho leapt up, heat burning her face. Standing over them, Georgette shook her head, a wide smile on her face.

Ziry pushed herself up more slowly. "I mean, I did take one of them out. Don't I deserve a celebratory kiss?" She winked at Georgette, laughing at the situation.

Chapter 34 - That's A Wrap
Ziry

Most of the wolves and witches left. Somehow the only deaths were the black witches. A group stayed behind to clean up the compound and search for more information.

"Okay," Ziry started. "We should get the dead bodies out of here. We can put them all in an area together and maybe use fire?" She turned to Cinthia.

"That can work. We just have to make sure to contain the flames and not start a forest fire."

Caroline came up next to her. "Two fire bugs and two water witches, just in case. An air witch to blow the smoke and smell straight up?"

Ziry searched the two women's faces. "Do the two of you have this? I'd like to start searching the offices."

Caroline nodded. "We have this."

Rho showed Ziry around. They ended up in one of the offices. Sitting on opposite sides of the desk, they searched through the documentation. Though she wanted to bundle Rho up and take her ... anywhere else, they both needed to finish this job.

The first office belonged to someone named Barry. He didn't have anything of use. Despite their seeming worthlessness, they put the papers into a box and moved on.

The next office had a plaque on the wall that read 'Kandi Purr.' Ziry shrugged at the name. Rho snarled. It was almost wolf-life ... very sexy. "She's the one who tried to kill you."

Ziry smirked. "Yeah, but who killed whom? That bitch had nothing on me."

"She threw you against a wall!"

"And? I'm a wolf, that's like playing a game."

Rho rolled her eyes. "You're awful."

With a snicker, Ziry realized she felt better than she had in days. She watched Rho for a few seconds, lost in her beauty, before getting back to the desk and papers. They needed to determine if anything was worth saving.

Rho's head snapped up. "Oh! Look at this. It describes shipments of the concoction. The black witches called it 'Power Heart.' Six distribution centers ... no names, no address, gah! This is useless!"

The discovery gave them new energy. With that vigor, they continued searching until after dinner.

Rho cupped Ziry's face, pulling her away from the documents. "Will you please take me away?

I've been held here for two weeks, I just want to see the inside of my apartment."

Guilt punched into Ziry. Why hadn't she thought of that? "Yes, of course. Let's go."

They found Caroline, working on searching one of the common rooms, and Ziry tapped her shoulder. "We're going to leave. Can we take one of the cars? I'm sure Rho can lead the way, or I have GPS."

Caroline nodded. "Yeah, but one thing." She faced Rho. "You said there were nine witches here including Sage?"

Rho nodded. "Yeah, why? How many bodies were left?"

"That's just it. There were four that had been mummified. Those bitches have no respect for anyone, not even their own ... though, the mummified bodies were easy to dispose of. There were four others. That's eight, not nine. We think one got away. We don't know if the recipe for the concoction went with whomever escaped. We got images. Ziry, do you recognize any missing from the ones who were in and out of the lab?"

She and Rho looked through the pictures. Rho grumbled. "It's Gabby, Gabby Dura. She was the one who spent all her time watching the pack house. She rarely went to the lab. I doubt she could replicate anything. Here's the thing: she knows how to sneak into the backyard. She's a danger to the wolves."

Anger burned through Ziry, but she knew there was nothing she could do right then.

Mazzy snarled low. "Not anymore she's not."

As Ziry and Rho headed to the car, they heard Mazzy calling Tamsin, letting her know about Gabby.

The drive into the city took longer than either of them wanted it to, given how tired they were. When they got to Rho's apartment building, they stumbled up to her unit, then collapsed on a couch. Ziry leaned over and gently kissed Rho. She wasn't going to, but after two weeks, she couldn't stop herself.

"Okay, you're tired. I'll control myself. You go to sleep, I'll stay here."

"Fuck that!" Rho said. "I've dreamt of having you back in my bed for two weeks. Why would I wait another night?"

A smile tugged at the side of Ziry's mouth. "Do you want to shower first?"

"Hmmm, you know, with how tired we are, it would be best for us to shower together. Anything else would just be unsafe." Rho leaned over and returned Ziry's kiss, letting one hand cup Ziry's head, the other wrap around her waist.

Their tongues re-met after two weeks of separation. Chills of want and desire coursed through Ziry's body. She slipped her hand under Rho's shirt, enjoying the velvet smooth skin. She reached Rho's lacy bra and rubbed her thumb over the perfect breast, feeling the tightening of her nipple.

Rho pulled away with a groan. "Shower, bed, fucking, sleep."

"Yes, ma'am," Ziry said, then leaned forward to lick her neck and suck on her ear lobe. Rho whimpered, pushing closer for more.

Ziry stood, pulling Rho with her. "Come with me, my delicious witch."

In the bathroom, Ziry turned the shower on so the water would warm up, then slowly stripped the clothes off Rho, kissing the exposed skin as it appeared. Once the amazing, beautiful witch was naked, she slid out of her own clothes, and they both moved into the therapeutically blissful warm shower, letting it wash away the dirt, grime, and the worst of the memories of the day.

Ziry picked up the shampoo, and started massaging it into Rho's short, brown, curly hair. She took time to ensure to clean and rinse, leaning down to kiss Rho deeply as the last of the shampoo sluiced away.

Rho turned them so Ziry was under the stream of warm water. Her skilled fingers worked through the tangles Ziry knew her hair must be in after the day she'd had. They faced each other, so to really get to all her hair, Rho had to rub her luscious body against her. Sliding a leg forward, Ziry rubbed her sex against Rho, loving how much of their bodies touched.

Once the water ran clear, she picked up the soap and, starting at the top, stroked every inch of what she was beginning to think was the most beautiful body she'd ever been with. As the water cleared away the soap from the breasts, Ziry licked, then dragged her teeth over each nipple.

She made sure to get between Rho's legs, then used a washcloth to clear away the suds. Unable to control herself, she gave Rho's ass a quick nip. The other woman squawked, then laughed.

When she finished, Rho breathed faster. "My turn."

"No, I want you in bed. Dry off, I'll be out in a minute."

Rho snarled but agreed. It only took a few moments to get herself sudsed then rinsed before she exited the shower to find a towel and quickly dry.

In the bedroom, Rho lay on her back, balanced on her elbows, a sultry smile on her face. Ziry selected a foot and took her time kissing up from Rho's shin to her knee. Her tongue traveled up her thigh, swirling and tasting. Rho breathing became ragged and rough as Ziry made it to the spot she'd been aiming for all night.

With a slow lick, she tasted how excited and ready Rho was for her, her musky smell tightening muscles low in Ziry, heat building within her.

Ziry's tongue flicked up to Rho's clit, then she sucked. She slid her fingers into the tight, slick canal ready for her attention. Her other hand glided up the silky smooth skin to Rho's chest, and Ziry was in heaven.

Rho moaned as she moved under her, pushing up into her mouth, begging for more. She arched up as her breath came in short bursts.

As quickly as they started, it wasn't long before Rho screamed out Ziry's name, body tightening around her, then she dropped back down to the bed.

Ziry crawled up to lie next to her, cradling Rho in her arms.

Rho gazed up, eyes barely open. "My turn?"

"Oh no, you sleep. We'll have plenty of time to do more later. Just let me hold you, my love."

Ziry froze for a moment, then decided she liked the sound of those words for this woman. She was pretty sure Rho was too tired to have heard them anyway. She reached down and pulled a blanket over them.

Just as she was about to fall asleep, Rho burrowed in deeper and mumbled, "Love you, too."

Chapter 35 - Brunch Or Bust
Tamsin

Tamsin knew she had to move on from the battle and give her pack some normalcy. She, Orin, and Georgette got up early to start their normal Sunday brunch. She stood at the stove making eggs, bacon, and hashbrowns. Her cooking team focused on the other parts of the feast.

Somehow, none of the wolves or witches that she and Ziry had taken to the black witch stronghold had died. A few were hurt, but everyone would live to fight another day.

Ziry had stayed behind to collect information. Cinthia, Mazzy, and Caroline were amongst the ones to join her to take care of the dead black witches and clear out the rooms to see if they could find any information about where they'd sent their concoction. The group that stayed was bigger than expected because it was spring break and many of them had the extra time.

Spring Break. The wedding—my wedding—is on Thursday. Glancing over her shoulder, Tamsin looked at Paige. Her fiancé sat with Tory—the two non-cookers tried to stay out from underfoot. A warmth bubbled in her at the thought that she and Paige were really going to marry in less than a week.

As the three cooks finished preparing the food, they brought most of it into the dining room, the area that fit the largest number of pack members. People slowly trudged down the stairs, tramped into the kitchen for coffee, then came into the larger room for Sunday brunch.

When the majority of the pack joined them, eating, talking, and laughing, Tamsin leaned back and took in her family. It was just about a year ago she'd flown in from Chicago to figure out why her aunt had died, and now she sat, alpha of these amazing wolves, amongst these wonderful people.

Down the table were two kids, Rainy and Stewart. They were the next generation of the pack. They were why everyone went out and fought for their land. Yes, protecting the people of Santa Cruz was important, but protecting these kids was everything.

"But I wanna wear a dress and toss flowers!" Stewart crossed his arms and his lower lip pouted out.

Rainy's face stiffened. "I'm the flower girl and you carry the rings. We've discussed this a ka-billion times!"

"I don't wanna wear the stupid suit. Your outfit is more comfortable." He scrunched up his face. "I'll carry the stupid rings if I can wear the dress."

The young girl snarled, "No. I won't wear the suit."

Bexlee sat across from them. Tamsin saw her trying not to laugh. "Why don't we ask Tamsin and Paige if you both can wear matching dresses? Maybe you can wear dresses with suit jackets, so you both have a piece from each other's outfits."

Tamsin looked at Paige and saw the amusement she felt on her partner's face. The two kids slowly scrunched up their faces and gazed at each other. Then Rainy, the clear leader of the two, turned towards the head of the table. "Tamsin, Paige, can we do what Bexlee said?"

She loved that the kids knew everyone had followed their discussion, that they were important to all of them. "Yes, sweetie, I think that would be perfect. I'll speak with Rho and see if she can take you two out shopping this week."

Smiles bloomed on both kids' faces.

Once that was decided, Tamsin searched the pack members in the room, then turned to Paige. "Did Ziry come home last night?"

Georgette, halfway down the table, snorted. "No. Didn't you see her and Rho?"

Tamsin shook her head. "Wait, what am I missing? Weren't they just partnering up to find the lab and witches?"

"Well, they definitely 'partnered up.'"

Tamsin smiled. "Well, in that case, I'm glad Ziry is happy. Though, she's heading home soon."

"Will she stay for the wedding?" Georgette asked.

Before Tamsin could answer, someone came in the front door. A moment later, Ziry and Rho entered the dining room. Ziry smiled. "I could smell the meal halfway across the city. Did you leave any for us?"

Two seats were cleared for them near where Tamsin sat. Once they'd started eating, Tamsin asked, "Did you learn anything about their liquid death yesterday?"

Ziry put down her fork and leaned back. "There were papers, but not details. There are six distribution centers in town, but no names, no addresses. They'd done a drop-off with the last of their supplies from the shell house the week before. There was nothing left to destroy, so that means, unless the distribution centers are found, the antidote will be needed at least until summer, if not through summer."

Maria sighed. "Well, at least Caroline and Mazzy are hard at work making the antidote. But six centers? That's rough."

Rho leaned forward. She looked a bit nervous. "You left early, before this was discovered. We think one of the black witches got away. The one that had been watching your pack house."

Tamsin forced her face to remain neutral, but inside she seethed. *Fucking black witches.* "Anything else I should know?"

"They know you keep your back gate to the park open. She's been sneaking in. She told the others in the coven. I don't know if she's told anyone else, but you need to be careful."

Down the table, Georgette snarled. "I'll set up a watch and make sure the door is locked when we're not out on a run. I'll also figure out a way to make sure it's locked when we are on a run. I don't relish the thought of someone coming in when we're all out. It isn't hard to figure out which night it's open."

Tamsin nodded. This witch was going to be trouble.

Chapter 36 - Long Walks On The Beach
Rho

It was Monday morning. Rho awoke before Ziry. She didn't want to wake up her wolf. Slipping from bed, she headed into the kitchen to start the coffee maker. Once she had a cup, she sat out on her small patio and thought about two nights before. The cool breeze and the singing of the birds centered her. So long underground hadn't done her well.

She remembered Ziry saying she loved her and was pretty sure she mumbled it back. They hadn't repeated the words since. Sunday had been too busy.

Do I want to tell her again? Does it matter? Her parents are coming to officiate Tamsin and Paige's wedding. Only an alpha can marry alpha wolves. And after the ceremony, they'll all be going back to South Dakota.

She sipped her coffee, enjoying the morning breeze. She loved Santa Cruz and the life she'd built but would happily follow Ziry to her home in South Dakota.

But that's crazy. Would she even want me? Am I putting the cart before the horse?

The sound of movement caught her attention, and then Ziry stepped out holding her own steaming mug of coffee, her usually perfect dark auburn hair a tangled mess atop her head. Rho smiled at the memory of how Ziry's hair got so messed up. She only wore a T-shirt that barely covered the light pink panties. When she sat in the other chair, the shirt slid up, giving Rho a clear view of Ziry's pale, well-muscled thighs.

Favorite outfit ever!

Ziry yawned and sipped from her mug. "Morning, sunshine. You're up early."

"Usually. I was just thinking about today, and the next few todays." She sighed and sipped her coffee. "I think I'm starting to miss you and you're still here."

Ziry lowered her mug, cupping it in both hands. "I know what you mean. I ache to get home to my pack. I miss my family, but my heart hurts thinking about leaving you. You've become my family, too."

Heat and desire rose in Rho. She decided she didn't care about the consequence, she was never one to be squeamish, and she wouldn't start now. Staring into Ziry's pale green eyes, she put her mug on the small table. Her heart beat faster and she licked her lips. "Ziry Sanch, I'm going to miss you with all my heart because you are my heart. Since you've come to Santa Cruz you've stolen it. I've completely fallen in love with you, and when you leave, I don't know what I'll do."

There, she'd said it, bared her soul. Let the universe do with her words what it would.

Ziry put her mug on the table and moved to kneel between Rho's legs. She slid her warm hands over Rho's, cool from the morning's chill. "When you were gone for all those days, I knew something was wrong. At the start, everyone said I was overreacting, but I was certain you wouldn't go that long without talking to me." A tremor in her voice. "I knew it because I couldn't go that long without talking to you. I spent each day missing your touch, your taste, your smile," she reached up and traced Rho's mouth, "your everything. It didn't take long for me to know that not only had I chosen you, so had my wolf. I've fantasized about stealing you away and taking you back home with me."

She stood and gently kissed Rho. When she backed away, Rho could see the anguish on her face. "I know your life is here. It's hard when a wolf has chosen the one they want. I only hope it hasn't gotten to the danger point."

"Danger point?" Rho frowned. What did that mean?

"It isn't anything we need to worry about, we're not mated. When a wolf finds a mate, the two connect on a deep level. It's almost as if they become one. The Colorado group has done some research on this. As long as this stays a fling, we should be fine."

"Wait, like, connected beyond love?" Rho sounded nervous and intrigued.

"Well, yeah. A metaphysical connection. I think it's rather beautiful."

Rho narrowed her eyes and was about to respond when Ziry's belly grumbled. Ziry smiled wide. "Why don't we head out for food? My parents arrive at eleven. We can pick them up after breakfast."

Rho sighed but agreed.

They found a diner and ordered breakfast. The entire time, Rho thought about what Ziry had told her. Finally, the other woman put down her fork. "What are you thinking? You've been so quiet. Did I do or say something wrong?"

Rho released the breath she'd been holding. "Witches can't live in a werewolf pack house. Even if I agree to relocate, move to South Dakota, where would I live?"

Ziry rolled her eyes. "You'd live with me. My pack is the trailblazer of the country. We were the first to get along with the witches after we had to band together to get rid of the black witches all those years ago. And now, if you really are considering this, then you'd live with us. Fuck the stupid rules."

Hope bubbled within Rho. "Do you need to double-check with your parents?"

"No, I don't need to ask them about this. I'll tell them if you're serious." Her green eyes glowed with excitement.

The plane landed early. When they pulled up to pick up Ziry's parents, Rho leapt out to offer ... either of them, the front seat.

Ziry got out of the driver's seat a bit more slowly and hugged her mom and dad. She was the female image of her dad, with the same color hair and eyes. Though her coloring matched her dad's, Ziry's hair was the same flowing waves as her mom's. The whole family seemed to have easy smiles.

Once the car was packed, they began the drive from the airport to pack house.

"... and this is Rho. She's been my partner in crime, figuring this all out."

"My daughter—willing to work with someone?" Her dad made a comical shocked face that Rho could see since she'd turned in the seat to face Ziry's parents in the back seat.

Ziry pursed her lips, holding back a laugh, but her eyes danced. "Rho, this is my dad, Jackson." Her head tilted towards the other occupant. "And this is my mom, Fran."

Fran reached out and squeezed Rho's shoulder. "I can tell there's more than 'just partners' here. The case is closed, and you're still together. Thank you for whatever it is you've been doing to keep our daughter happy. Her mood seems lighter."

Rho saw Ziry blushing.

Ziry's eyes danced, though her face clashed with her hair it was so bright. "Yes, Mom, Dad, I've been trying to convince Rho to come home with me. Instead of her finding a wolf to bring home, I've found a witch I want to have follow *me*. She's worried because around here they still don't let witches live in their pack house."

Fran guffawed, and Jackson scoffed. He said, "If you and my daughter decide to mate, you'll live wherever she lives. Since she's the next alpha of our pack, that's the pack house. Anything else is just ridiculous. Now, how long until we get to see Tamsin and her mate? We'd like to see her now that she's all grown up."

Rho was gob-smacked at how easy that had all been.

The drive was blissfully quick. They seemed to miss most of the ugly traffic. Once they got to the pack house, they found Tamsin and Paige in the living room. With them were Joyce and Orin. Maria and Blake, Joyce's daughter, sat on a love seat, Maria on her laptop, Blake reading a book.

Both Jackson and Fran stopped and gazed at them. Orin slowly stood, tears starting to fall from his eyes. "Is it all true? The pack wasn't all killed? I mean, I know what Joyce told me, but I was too scared. I'd lived too long to challenge what had been put in my mind."

Jackson walked up to Orin and wrapped him in a hug. "Orin! My boy. It's been too long. We spent so much time looking for you. I'm glad to see you again."

Joyce moved to Fran to collect a similar hug.

A bit confused, Rho searched the misty faces. Not wanting to disturb them, Rho sought out the others in the room. Blake looked both happy and sad for her mom. When she saw Rho watching, she smiled. "Black witches destroyed their pack when they were kids. Mom was a teen, but Orin was really young, Stewart's age. Orin just recently learned that anyone from his pack survived."

Something in Rho broke at the hurt of a young boy separated from his family. She remembered the discussion of the black witches who had spoken so casually about killing the parents of young kids. She wanted to go back and take a larger part in the destruction of the bitches who'd taken her captive. They were all awful.

As the group sat to catch up, she headed out to the backyard. The day was warm, and she sat in a reclining chair, enjoying the heat of the sun. The scent of flowers and the song of the birds were a balm to her soul. Being out here she felt like she wasn't intruding on whatever reunion was happening inside. No one made her feel like an unwanted guest, but they needed time and space.

After a few minutes, Georgette came out and sat next to her. "How are you doing?"

Rho smiled. "I'm good. So much has happened since my captivity, it's nice to be out here, away from all the chaos."

"I get that. Do you want me to leave?"

Rho thought about the question then shook her head. "Unlike the black witches, you have no desire to manipulate or change me. It's rather refreshing, actually."

"Well, you know, if you want any of that, just ask."

Rho laughed. As they sat and enjoyed the afternoon in companionable silence. A peace overcame her. She hadn't had time to just be in tune with herself and nature—unworried about everything—for weeks.

She felt she could doze off when Georgette's hand on her arm startled her. The other woman spoke so softly, Rho almost missed the words. "Stay still, don't react. Pretend to be asleep. I've informed Tamsin. She's bringing backup. We're safe."

Slitting her eyes open, Rho tried to look around the backyard, but she couldn't see anything. She also didn't hear anything. Then she saw a shadow waver against the fence that shouldn't be there. *It's fucking Gabby, the bitch. Well, black witches have their tricks, but so do I!*

She hadn't used much of her magic in weeks. She'd shown Sage how she could cause the wind to blow, but watching the black witches freeze people in boxes of air, hell, she could do that. Homing in on Gabby, she focused and with a push of her will froze the black witch in her tracks.

Next to her, Georgette jerked, looking around. When she saw Gabby, her brow furrowed. "Did you do something? Her scent disappeared and she's frozen."

"I froze the air around her. I'm tired of doing nothing, Georgette. I'm in this fight. I'm a witch. I have powers. Now she's stuck until I release her or run out of power. I can hold her for about an hour." She felt empowered to finally be doing something, not sitting back observing or being managed.

Tamsin came out with the rest of the people who'd been in the living room. Rho filled her in. Tamsin narrowed her eyes at the black witch in consideration. "Can you or we move her? Put her in a cell? Can we make it safe to keep her?"

Rho nodded, feeling like one of the team. "You can move her. I can restrict the air to as close around her as needed. But in an hour she'll have access to whatever power she has stored up. I'm guessing she's at full capacity right now."

The others nodded. Jackson considered her. "Is there much more information you expect to get from her?"

Tamsin sighed. "Probably not. I'm just tired of all the death." *So am I, so am I. But with her alive, death will continue on an exponential scale.*

Jackson nodded as if he'd heard Rho's thoughts. "Well, how about as an early wedding gift we take care of her for you? You all go in—except for Rho. I'll need her. We'll drag the bitch ... I mean, black witch out to the woods, and you'll never have to worry about her again."

Tamsin shook her head. "I can't ask you to do that."

Paige put a hand on her mate's shoulder. "Let him, love. It's a gift."

Once it was decided, the others went inside, and Rho, Fran, and Jackson maneuvered Gabby into the woods through the larger door meant for people, versus the gate the wolves usually used.

They followed the path until they were well away from civilization, and then Jackson asked her to release the witch.

Rho released the witch, Fran holding her in a hug.

"You fucking traitor, conspiring with the fucking dogs!"

Before Gabby could get another word out, Jackson reached over and snapped her neck. She was so focused on spitting insults at Rho, she ignored the real threat in the woods.

The relief as the last of the people who knew the way to make the heart attack concoction expired made Rho feel like she could fly.

Jackson wrapped an arm around Rho. "I like you. I think you'll make an excellent addition to our family."

Chapter 37 - I Do!
Ziry

After Rho and her parents had taken care of the last black witch, a lightness overtook everyone. It felt like things were finally over. Ziry had packed up her room. The job was over.

Since she remained in Santa Cruz for the wedding, she decided to shift her accommodations to Rho's place; she was pretty much staying there anyway. That gave the pack one more room to fill with other guests, including her parents, who took her room.

As the days of spring break for the college slipped by, Ziry focused on other things in the city. She visited the lab and Mazzy and Caroline demonstrated how they created the antidote with a combination of science and magic. They worked as fast as they could, sending their solution out to any place the black witches may hit.

She also spent time with Rho, making sure the other woman really wanted to relocate. "There will be snow and no ocean, you know."

Rho bumped into her as they sat on the bed, naked after the shower. "I grew up in Texas in the middle of the state. No ocean there. I'll be fine."

"Right, but that doesn't address the snow, or the fact that it isn't easy being a personal shopper in a state without the socialite crowd."

Rho threw her head back and laughed. "I think I can figure out how to morph my skills into something else: event planner, photographer ... Or, you know, private investigator."

Amusement bubbled in Ziry. "We could open up a firm together." She got up and found the panties and bra for under the dress she'd be wearing to the wedding.

"Yes! I would love that." Rho gazed at her, the look a mixture of excitement for the idea of working together and lust as she watched Ziry slowly hook the lacy bra.

Rho finally managed to get herself put together as well. She wore a deep purple sleeveless dress that ended mid-thigh. The A-line cut accentuated her lovely figure. Ziry had a silk, rust-colored, draped dress that clung to her body as it fell just past her knees. The complementary colors looked like bright flowers next to each other.

Not having to shop is a real advantage to sleeping with ... and loving, a personal shopper.

The pack had rented a hall. When they arrived, Jett and Katt stood outside, welcoming people to the venue. Jett must have recently done her hair because the purple tips practically glowed in the sun.

"Did you see how the two of them had matching A-line dresses? Jett's was sleeveless with the high neckline and Katt's had the longer sleeves and lower V-neck. They go with the deep wine color. Not identical, but they do go together well."

Ziry narrowed her eyes. "How many people here did you dress?"

Rho just smiled and sauntered into the hall.

Inside, chairs lined both sides of a flower-lined path. The flowers to the left started at a dark orange. In an ombre effect, they morphed to a light orange and then ended in white. The center aisle was white to the other side. The right-side chairs had a similar ombre with flowers starting off a dark pink and flowing to fuchsia.

I love the nod to the lesbian flag. Rho reached over and squeezed her hand, smiling at the sight.

They'd arrived a bit early and nearly half the seats were taken. Ziry steered Rho toward the orange flower side.

Up front, Paige stood next to an arbor covered in similar flowers as the chairs. She wore a white suit with a tie in the colors of the lesbian flag. Next to her stood Connie and Maria. Under the arbor was

Ziry's mom wearing a purple dress, similar in style to her own.

Rho leaned over. "I've been to a lot of weddings, but I'm not clear why your mom had to come out to officiate this wedding."

Ziry took in the excited exuberance of the people around her. It wasn't often she could experience so much joy from so many people. "In wolf culture, a werewolf pair can be married in the same way any could do, but the alphas have a bit more that needs to go into the ceremony. We also like to have an alpha marry us. It makes our wolves preen."

"Is that why Maria and Blake had a second ceremony back in January?"

Ziry narrowed her eyes as she gazed at all the colorful clothes—it was all so pretty. "I didn't know they did, but yeah, that would make sense. If they had a first ceremony in the human way, they'd want one with Tamsin officiating, as well."

Over the next quarter hour, the seats around them filled. She spent that time explaining more of the history and traditions of the wedding ceremony to Rho, so she'd know what to watch for. At some signal neither of them heard or saw, the music from a live quartet began.

It began with Stewart. He wore an orange dress with a matching sports coat. He walked to the end and sat down between Bexlee and Toby, his father. Rainy was next, in a fuchsia dress and matching sports coat. She traversed the aisle throwing white rose petals. When she got to the end, she sat on the right side next to her mom.

It was time for the people standing up on Tamsin's side, Maria and Tory. From what Ziry remembered, Maria was one of Tamsin's idols growing up, and Tory was someone she hung out with a lot, being so close in age.

As the two passed, wearing cream dresses, Ziry turned to Rho. Rho had helped with all the outfits for the wedding party. "Do you know who's walking with Tamsin down the aisle?"

This was a big question. Both her parents, as well as her uncle and aunt, had passed away. Having an elder there to give you away was very important to the ceremony, more so than in the human ones.

Rho tilted her head. "Yeah, actually, it surprised me when I heard Tamsin was being 'given' to Paige since Tamsin is the alpha and Paige is submissive. I guess Cinthia, though a witch, has been part of the family her whole life. Always in family ceremonies."

Ziry shook her head. "It has to be a wolf."

Before Rho could explain, the bridal procession music started. Tamsin, wearing a beautiful fitted white dress that flared past her hips, entered the hall. She stood between Cinthia and Georgette. The three slowly marched down the aisle to the audible gasps of the onlookers.

The rules are changing. Happiness bubbled in her at the thought.

When they got to the end of the aisle, Ziry's mom nodded once. "Who brings forth and offers Tamsin Hath, alpha of the Pacific Pack, to Paige Glass, to mate, to bond, to together lead such a strong and noble group of wolves?"

The words held power, and there was a buzzing in the air. Traditionally, one person answered. Ziry's breath caught, wondering what would happen next. She leaned forward and saw many others mirroring her actions.

Cinthia's words rang out, and she too spoke with command, filling the room with magic. "I, Cinthia Olson, stand for Tamsin's Aunt, her Uncle, and her parents. Her family has passed, but I knew them all well. I've helped raise her, and as such, I have the honor and privilege of accepting this duty. Tamsin, go forth in peace and tranquility and find your new path with Paige."

The words reverberated throughout the room. Once the last echo cleared, a stillness blanked the spectators.

"I, too, have the duty and honor of bringing Tamsin forward." Georgette started, pride emanating from her. "I have been her pack mate, friend, and sister her whole life. I have seen her grow from a pup to the brilliant leader she is today, and with all my heart I am privileged to help bring her from alpha to alpha pair. Tamsin, join your lovely life partner and may your joy only bring more love and life to us all." Georgette's truth flowed over them all.

Mom smiled. "You two may sit. Tamsin, please step forward." The two brides stood facing each other, smiling, beautiful. "The union of two wolves is a serious joining. Our wolves love deeply. Once they've found the one they want, their hearts are attached for life. These two are lucky enough to have found each other. Any who have had the privilege of spending time with them know that their love is true and pure. I am excited to see what their future will bring. Now, Paige, did you prepare something?"

Paige nodded. "As a journalist you would hope this would be good, but with so much to say, I'm just hoping to get something out." As she dabbed at her eyes, the people in the crowd chuckled. "I've always been alone. I grew up in foster care, and being part of a family was this weird dream I never thought would become a reality. Then, off on a case, writing up a story, I was attacked. As much as I don't want to bring in those ... well, you all know, they did bring me you." She waved her hand at the audience. "And you." She lifted her hand and rested it on Tamsin's chest, just below her shoulder.

After a moment, she continued. "As awful as the night was, I'd do it a million times to have gained the family and friends I've gotten. I mean, the love is good and all, but all of it. I love you all. And Tamsin ... you most of all. I love you, every day, every minute, every second. I can't believe I found someone so amazing who loves me back."

Her hand dropped, and she shrugged. "What else is there to say? My life is so different, so much better, and I'm so much happier. I love you."

All around Ziry, people dabbed their eyes. Next to her Rho reached over to squeeze her knee. *Is there a ceremony like this in our future?*

Mom smiled, her pride filling the room. She spoke quietly to Paige. "You did good." Then louder, "Tamsin, your turn."

The smile on Tamsin's face looked as if it couldn't get any bigger. "I'm supposed to follow that? Oy! Okay." She reached out for Paige's hands, and Ziry saw her close her eyes for a moment before opening them. "Paige, you entered my life like a whirlwind of passion and excitement. I came to Santa Cruz with a mission. I had been living a numb life and planned on continuing to do so. You broke through that, reminding me how to live and love. You showed me that I needed more than survival. I needed life and color and people who cared for me. If it hadn't been for you, I'd still be living half a life, secretly miserable. Because of you, I'm filled with peace and love, surrounded by the most amazing family, and ready to soar. I love you more every day, and it excites me to see what will come next. Thank you for being you and challenging me to be better every day. I love you,

Paige." It looked like she wanted to say more but couldn't.

Tamsin slid her arms around Paige's neck.

Mom cleared her throat. "One sec."

Tamsin smiled wide. "If I must." She let her hands drop and the crowd tittered.

Mom searched Tamsin's face then nodded. "Do you, Paige Glass, take Tamsin Hath to be your mate for all time?"

"I do!"

Mom smiled. "And do you, Tamsin Hath, take Paige Glass to be your mate for all time?"

The joy within Tamsin burst throughout the room. "I do!"

Mom nodded. "With the exchanging of vows, the bond of the mate is done. These two are as one, and as one they will be from now until death. Be it ill or well, sorrow or joy, hunt or play, together they will be a unit. With these words, the mating of Tamsin Hath and Paige Glass is official. Will Stewart Court bring up the rings?"

Stewart popped up and presented the pillow.

First Paige and then Tamsin collected a ring to slip on the other woman's finger.

Again, the power radiated out, warm and electric, and the crowd cheered.

"Let all here rejoice in the joining of two hearts as humans and wolves, they become one unit. Now, you may kiss your bride."

And Tamsin did.

Chapter 38 - Saying Goodbye!
Rho

The reception for the wedding was beautiful. Round tables with white linen were scattered around the room. A dance floor was open at one end, and Rainy and Stew already danced, not patient enough to wait for the food.

Each table had a bouquet of flowers, some wolf-shaped confetti, and a small candle. There were also tall glass jars with wine that wait staff replaced as they emptied.

The crowning display was the wedding cake. Rho had been there when it had been ordered. Two wolves, one red, one white, howling at a moon, suspended over a large tree. The cake artist had done a fantastic job of capturing the lifelike qualities of the wolves. The red wolf was a chocolate mocha, the white wolf spiced cake with pistachio. The tree was a caramel with baked apple. If anyone dared ask for a slice of moon, it was s'mores flavored.

Rho sipped her wine as the first course, a salad and jumbo scallop, was delivered. Emotions roiled in her. She could feel the magic throughout the ceremony. She wasn't sure if it was because she was a witch, or because she had an affinity towards animal magic, but it enchanted her.

She played back the ceremony and the words, letting them seep into her bones as she slowly ate her food and sipped her wine.

A warm hand on her forearm got her attention. Next to her, Ziry smiled. "A penny for your thoughts."

"I don't know if I want a penny, but I'd take a kiss."

A huge smile blossomed on the other woman's face, exactly as Rho had hoped. Ziry leaned over and gave her a chaste kiss. "Payment enough?"

"For now. I'll exact a better toll from you later."

"Hmm," she whispered, leaning in to lightly lick the edge of Rho's ear. Rho shivered in anticipation. "Sounds like the kind of threat I like, my sexy witch."

"I've been playing back the ceremony. It was magical ... literally. Do you know the amount of magic involved?"

"To some extent. I could feel the power. I know how binding all of the parts are. Did it worry you? Are you changing your mind?"

For a few moments, Rho had no idea what she was talking about. Then it hit her. "About South Dakota? No. I love you and your family is wonderful. The thought of not having you around hurts me here." She rubbed her chest.

Ziry scooted her chair closer and slipped an arm around Rho's shoulders. "Good. I may have started to panic."

Rho leaned her head on Ziry's shoulder. "The ceremony was lovely, that's all."

The meal continued for a few more courses, and then there was a break. The cake would be cut after people had time to move around and let the food settle. Tamsin and Paige got up to socialize.

Paige made it over to their table. They both stood to give her a hug.

Rho beamed at her. "It was fantastic, I had no idea what to expect!"

Paige snorted. "You weren't the only one. I knew the basics from the walk-through, but you're not the only one new to werewolf culture. The power that flowed through the ceremony, gah! But being in the center of it all, I loved it. I love Tamsin, but I don't think I'd want to do it again. Maybe watch it. Am I invited to your wedding?"

Ice cold water wouldn't have been as shocking. Not that Ziry couldn't have thought her and Rho's relationship through to that conclusion, but they'd only known each other a short while.

Rho reacted faster than she could. "Any wedding I'm in, you are definitely invited to, punk wolf!"

Paige laughed.

Ziry shook her head at the two of them. "So, are you and Tamsin off on a honeymoon? Where are you going?"

Paige slumped a bit before finding Tamsin in the crowd. "Since she teaches, we're waiting until June. Then we're planning on visiting Paris and London. She wants to visit the London pack. She knows the alpha there, though they've never met in person. Beyond that, who knows. Maybe we'll see more of the UK."

Rho sighed. "That all sounds amazing. I bet it'll be lovely and relaxing. You'll have to tell us all about it."

"Will do. Now, I must finish making my rounds so we can get to the cake!"

Ziry gave her one more hug before Paige slipped away. Ziry held her hand out to Rho. "Care to dance."

Rho smiled wide. "I'd love to."

Ziry slipped her arms around the most beautiful woman in the room, and they danced. After a few minutes, Rho looked out and they both saw Tamsin and Paige dancing. "I just can't believe how lucky they are to be taking that trip. They'll be globe-trotting!"

With a bit of a squeeze and a turn on the dance floor, Ziry took Rho for a spin. "They deserve it after everything that's happened here. Though, if you want to travel ... If we're working together in a detective firm, then we can set our own vacation schedule. You name the place, and we're off."

Rho's eyes shone with excitement. "You know, Ziry Sanch, I just may love you."

"That's good, Rho Mercer, because I love you, too."

Find the Next Book – a Novella!

Tamsin and Paige got married!

Read about their Honey Moon here:

https://mybook.to/HoneyMoon

Where to Find Harlowe Frost

Thanks for reading!

Find more of my books on my website:

http://hannahwillowauthor.com

You can also find me on:
Twitter: @hannahwillow217
Instagram: @hannahwillow217
Facebook Hannah Willow

About the Author

Harlowe Frost has been a teacher at both the high school and college level. Her parents instilled a love of reading from a young age. She grew up in the queer community. Her favorite genre growing up was fantasy and science fiction, that is, until she discovered urban fantasy and paranormal romance. What she never found in those books was the diversity in background, gender identity, and sexuality she saw in the people around her. She decided if she couldn't find that in what she read, then she would write it herself. This started her writing paranormal romance with a LGBTQ+ background